C...

The confessio... of the play. Ni... his usual confi...

At about l... , Titus casually strolled on stage. He sniffed carefully around and then decided that the upholstered arm of the settee was the best vantage point. He leapt up gracefully and got into position. Then he turned and stared at Nigel.

He stared. He kept still. He remembered what Lindy had said about blending, but it was a little difficult for a magnificent black and white short-haired cat to blend successfully.

He sat there throughout the whole speech, staring, dignified, enigmatic, ears pricked at such an angle that he looked as though he were listening politely to a vaguely amiable idiot.

Nigel fought back. His voice grew louder, his projection more deliberate. The sweat glistened on his forehead.

Then Titus yawned, a small pink-mouthed yawn of delicate boredom. The audience collapsed in laughter.

from *Curtain Call*

These CAT STORIES were originally published in the following magazines:

ESMERALDA – *Woman's Realm, 1959*
THIS MAN IS MINE – *Mother*, 1965
TUFTY'S HORSE – *Parents*, 1966
XINIA AND THE WITCH – *Favourite Story*, 1975
TRAVELS WITH INKY PACKER – *Woman's Realm*, 1978
THE CAT FROM NEXT DOOR – *Woman's Realm*, 1980
CURTAIN CALL – *My Weekly, 1981*

Illustrations by Marilyn Day

CAT STORIES

Stella Whitelaw

Stella Whitelaw

Hamlyn Paperbacks

CAT STORIES

ISBN 0 600 20229 1

First published in volume form in Great Britain 1981
by Hamlyn Paperbacks

Hamlyn Paperbacks are published by
The Hamlyn Publishing Group Ltd,
Astronaut House,
Feltham,
Middlesex, England

(Paperback Division: Hamlyn Paperbacks,
Banda House, Cambridge Grove,
Hammersmith, London W6 OLE)

Reproduced, printed and bound in Great Britain by
Hazell Watson & Viney Ltd, Aylesbury, Bucks

CONTENTS

To Diana, daughter dear

1 TRAVELS WITH INKY PACKER

Inky was an extraordinarily beautiful, pure white, long-haired, pedigree Persian. She had vivid blue eyes and exactly the right short nose, full cheeks and broad muzzle. She lived at Russets, Culimore Crescent with the Packers. It was a large, comfortable house, the kind estate agents describe as 'a highly desirable residence'.

Inky could have lived a pampered existence with a cushion to sleep on, daily grooming, limitless minced chicken, and nothing more exhausting to do than stretch herself luxuriously at the occasional cat show.

But Inky, right from kittenhood, developed some odd habits. For a start she preferred to be thought human and rapidly developed a liking for many human-type occupations. She regularly went shopping every morning, paying a call at each of the various establishments in the High Street, leaving the Chinese take-away and the fish and chip shop until last.

Twice a week she went to the Public Library and browsed round the shelves. She particularly liked the crime section which had quite a different smell. She soon became addicted to the television in the evening, but turned her back and went to sleep if a repeat was being shown.

She knew her way round the neighbourhood and there was hardly a building with an open door or window that she had not visited. Exclusiveness did not deter her. She preferred eating out, and several times strolled nonchalantly into a very posh restaurant, though she was soon lulled to sleep by the warmth of the place, and curled up on a stool at the cocktail bar.

She also liked a good play, and the bright lights of the local theatre lured her to an evening performance. It took two programme sellers ten minutes to coax her out from under the seats. Inky took umbrage at this total lack of understanding and retreated to the cinema where she sat through *A Hundred and One Dalmations* for the third time, which is saying something for a cat.

But she was a happy wanderer, and the Packer family became quite used to telephone calls from a faintly bewildered librarian.

'Miss Packer? We've got your cat here at the library again. Could you come and collect her? We don't like to just turn her out into the street.'

Elaine Packer would take the car down to the library and scoop the errant book-lover into her arms.

'Inky Packer,' she would say severely. 'Stop looking so lost and helpless. You know your way home perfectly well.'

Of course Inky knew her way home. She knew her way everywhere. But she would never pass up the chance of a ride in the car. She stood on the front seat with her paws on the dashboard ledge, her vivid blue eyes alert for any jay-walkers.

The other Packers, that is, George Packer and his daughter, Elaine, were resigned to Inky's wanderings until the episode of the hospital.

Inky could not have gone off at a worse time. George Packer worked for an advertising firm which had alternately grown and been taken over, grown and been taken over again. With this last takeover, he had an uneasy feeling that his style did not fit the trendy image of the present organisation, New Views Inc. George always believed in the products he advertised, and some of his accounts were very long-standing. He could not see himself promoting some tasteless product simply for a fast profit.

The word redundant had not exactly been mentioned but it hovered over his iron-grey head like a neon sign. Redundancy would not be that disastrous, but Russets cost a lot to run, there was still the mortgage to pay off, and jobs were not easy to find at his age. Fortunately Elaine was a thrifty housekeeper, and never thought of eating out or spending money on clothes.

Elaine, too, had her problems. But she did not say a word to her father for fear of hurting his feelings. She had taken over the reins of the household at seventeen when her mother died of an unexplained virus infection. Then it had seemed the right thing to do. She had no career in mind and was content to run the house and garden. But now she was almost twenty-eight, and when the children next door suddenly grew from Brownies into brides she began to feel restless.

There was very little she could do except run a household. She had not been trained for anything. But the urge to get away and do something on her own was certainly part of the reason for her restlessness.

Mr Packer invited Clive Hilton, Managing Director of New Views Inc. to supper. He had some strange idea that if he could show the young man the solid background and comfort of his home, Clive Hilton might feel less like casting him out into the street.

But it was also the day Elaine had arranged to go for an interview for a job. She had answered an advertisement for a housekeeper to a wealthy titled family with a large estate in Norfolk. It meant a long drive there and back. She wanted to look her best, so much of the evening beforehand was spent washing and setting her hair and pressing her best dress and jacket.

It was no wonder Inky decided to explore further afield. There was simply no one to talk to, and certainly too much fussing going on for one visitor. It was best to keep out of the way on such occasions.

Elaine did most of the meal before she left. The chocolate mousse was put to set in the refrigerator, the sauce for the prawn cocktail was ready mixed, the chicken casserole and vegetables sat in the automatic oven waiting to be switched on electronically.

'Now Inky, you've got to be a good girl while I'm away,' said Elaine to the white Persian. 'No going off anywhere.'

Inky looked at Elaine with blank astonishment. What me? Never. She pounded a little circle on Elaine's dressing stool and curled up for a snooze. She had every intention of remaining there for as long as it took Elaine to drive down the road.

The interview went well, and despite her lack of references Elaine felt she had a good chance of getting the job. But she hit the evening traffic and the return drive took far longer than she expected. She flew into the house. She had very little time to get everything ready.

The chicken casserole was definitely overcooked; the chocolate mousse slipped as she took it out of the refrigerator to decorate and slid untidily up the sides of the cut-glass bowl; and the mayonnaise, made in haste, had curdled. She was just making some more when Clive Hilton arrived.

Clive Hilton was a quiet young man in his early thirties, his horn-rimmed glasses hiding the determination and burning ambition in his eyes. He had built up New Ideas Inc. himself and was set on success. He had no room for old-fashioned operators like George Packer, and he was going to have to tell him tonight.

'I'm terribly sorry,' said Elaine, tucking wisps of hair behind her ears. 'Supper's going to be a bit late. I was delayed. Would you like to have a glass of sherry first?'

Despite the generous schooners of dry sherry, Elaine's supper was not memorable. George Packer could not think what had happened to his normally efficient daughter. The table was not even laid properly – no side plates and not so much as a daisy for a floral centrepiece.

They were trying to take Clive's mind off the dry chicken with conversation, when the telephone rang. A loud voice resounded against Elaine's ear-drums.

'One of my nurses tells me that this flea-ridden creature padding round my wards belongs to the Packers in Culimore Crescent,' she barked. 'Would you please come and remove it at once.'

'Inky hasn't got fleas,' said Elaine, not caring if Clive Hilton did hear.

'Anything that has fur and moves has got fleas,' said the

matron. 'You've got fifteen minutes to come and collect your animal, or I will telephone for the vet.'

The matron's voice was indeed threatening, and Elaine found that her hand was trembling slightly as she put the telephone down.

'That was the hospital,' said Elaine. 'Inky's visiting out of hours. I'll have to go and fetch her. I hope you don't mind having your mousse without any cream on top . . . '

And it was that evening the family car went on strike and refused to start. Try as she could, Elaine could not get any life out of it. The engine turned over with an unresponsive whine. She began to panic, remembering the fifteen-minute deadline and the fate that awaited her fluffy beauty.

Elaine felt the perspiration breaking out as she struggled with the starter.

'Having trouble?' inquired Clive owlishly.

'I've got to get to Inky,' said Elaine desperately. 'They're going to send for the vet.'

'We'd better go in my car then.'

The ward sister had shut Inky into the sluice room. Inky was quite indignant about it. She had come to visit the patients, not an unresponsive collection of bedpans. Still, it was clean. She sat on the floor licking her fur into place, waiting for Elaine to collect her in the car.

'So this is Inky,' said Clive, amused.

'Inky Packer,' said Elaine, lifting the cat up with one hand. Inky hung there, eyes closed, feigning a dreadful incurable illness. 'You bad, bad thing. I'm fed up with having to come and rescue you. Why can't you stay at home and catch mice?'

Inky shuddered at the word. However, she recovered when she saw the size and make of Clive's car, and forgot her indisposition enough to purr ecstatically while exploring the innards of the vehicle.

'Can't you get your cat to keep still?' asked Clive. 'It's a little unnerving having to drive with that thing leaping about.'

'She's enjoying it,' said Elaine. 'She likes your car. She's never been in a Mercedes before.'

'I'm glad she likes it, but I'd rather she sat on your lap.'

Elaine managed to extract Inky from the glove compartment and sat her forcibly on her knee. Inky trampled enthusiastically, her claws going through the thin material of Elaine's dress. Elaine gritted her teeth . . . after all, Clive had been very kind.

'Does your cat go wandering often?' Clive asked.

'Yes, but I know why she does it,' said Elaine with feeling. 'She just wants to get out and see the world.'

'Do I detect the stirrings of a rebellion in the homestead?'

'You do,' said Elaine, glad to have someone to tell. 'I've looked after my father for over ten years. I just feel it's time I started doing something of my own. I've got to get away.'

Clive Hilton was ruthless when it came to decisions, but even he could not see a man losing both job and daughter on the same evening. So he said nothing to George, but accepted Elaine's invitation to return for supper another evening before she took up a post.

This time her preparations were well in advance, and she set the table perfectly with matching candles and flowers. She also looked very pretty. A letter that morning confirming the job had given her a new sparkle. But she had yet to tell her father.

Just as Elaine was about to serve the salmon soufflé, the telephone rang. It was the local librarian.

'Oh dear, not Inky again,' said Elaine, exasperated. 'Would you mind keeping her for another ten minutes or my soufflé will collapse?'

'Oh, she isn't here,' explained the librarian. 'I just thought I ought to let you know that I saw her boarding a 507 bus to Kestram.'

Clive was very understanding about the supper. 'This is getting to be a habit,' he said, starting the Mercedes. 'Do you know the 507 route?'

'Vaguely,' said Elaine anxiously. 'I do hope she's all right. She'll be so frightened. She's never been on a bus before.'

'If I know Inky at all, she won't be in the least put out.

She's probably sitting up with the driver by now.'

'I hope she doesn't jump off anywhere.'

'What, and miss seeing the terminus? You bet she won't. That little lady can take care of herself. She'll land squarely on all four feet.'

Inky landed all right. They found her in the drivers' canteen sampling bus company milk. She'd had a lovely time. Buses were far more fun than that Mercedes. However, she was tired and quite happy to curl up on Elaine's lap for the drive home.

Seeing the contented look on Inky's face gave Clive an idea.

'I'm going to put Inky into advertising,' he announced.

Elaine stared at Clive in horror. 'Not cat food,' she said, appalled.

'Of course not. Tourism. I've a series of television ads to make for the American market to promote package tours to England. Who better than Inky, our happy wanderer, to show them around? Imagine . . . Inky at Edinburgh . . . Inky at Stratford-on-Avon . . . Inky at the Changing of the Guard . . . Inky meeting Concorde. . . !'

So Inky went on the box. She took to it like a duck to water. Filming held no terrors for her. And it meant lots of lovely travelling. George Packer became her business manager and Elaine, after sending a letter of regret to Norfolk, was Inky's personal assistant and travelling companion.

Clive supervised the American advertisements himself so it meant he saw a lot of Elaine. She grew prettier and prettier. One evening when they were at Land's End he asked her to marry him. She did not say yes at first, though she knew she would eventually. She had a little wandering of her own to do first. . . .

2 XINIA AND THE WITCH

Xinia was small, fluffy, predominantly marmalade in colour and inclined to be overweight. She did not know this as she was completely colourblind and disinclined to face facts. She thought herself to be a sleek cat, black as a raven's wing and destined by Fate to ride forever on the back of a broomstick.

It was the broomstick fixation that led Xinia to wander. She had had four homes in three years. They were mostly on lonely, isolated hill farms where you might expect a witch to lurk. But each time Xinia's hopes of finding one were doomed to disappointment, and so she decided to move on once again.

She moved on to Tupminster, a small village tucked away in the Cotswolds, green and growing, but still full of charm. There was a row of old farm labourers' cottages by the road leading into the village which had been turned into trendy weekend homes. The end cottage had more garden than the rest, and on her knees in the middle of the front path was a gorgeous female creature.

She was slim, willowy, with skin like fresh cream, cheeks flushed with her exertions at gardening, and a cascade of glossy black hair hanging down her back. At least Xinia thought it was glossy black hair, but really it was amber-blonde, with red and gold streaks that were a photographer's delight.

The young woman put down a trowel and began to leaf

through a clutch of seed packets. 'Virginia stock, Godetia, Candytuft, Gloxinias . . . ' she began to chant in a low voice.

As soon as Xinia heard her name called she leapt into action. Hello, new home! She threw herself enthusiastically into the young woman's arms, purring, pawing and generally making a nuisance of herself.

'Hello, pussy. Where did you come from?' the woman asked, removing her gardening gloves in order to give Xinia a friendly stroke.

Between purrs and chin-licking with her small, rough tongue, Xinia noted this refinement with some satisfaction. This was obviously the very nicest kind of witch. Xinia trampled happily over the scattered seed packets and then threw herself back into the witch's arms. Home number five was settled.

'Heavens, keep still, you funny little thing,' the young woman laughed, trying to free her hair from Xinia's claws. 'I'm not a bed and I don't need a bath. But I do think it's coffee time, don't you?'

Coffee might have magical properties but any time was milk time, so Xinia followed the young woman indoors, carefully keeping her long fluffy tail out of the way of the girl's bare feet. Bare feet, thought Xinia, were quite an improvement. Most witches wore the most awful heavy black boots with sharp, painful heels.

Sally Jenkins put her percolator on the stove and then opened the refrigerator door to get out some milk.

Xinia's amber-flecked green eyes widened with astonishment. Inside the door the milk was actually standing up, all by itself, in tall round shapes! It was quite amazing. Xinia was used to watching milk squirting from those stupid brown animals and being slopped around in pails. But here it was actually standing up in regular shapes inside this cupboard. Xinia held her breath, expecting the milk to suddenly collapse and spill all over the floor.

Sally poured some milk into a saucer and put it down for the cat. 'There you are, pussy,' she murmured absent-mindedly. She look a letter from her pocket and began reading it as she stirred her coffee. The letter looked as though it had been read many times. Sally gave a small quivering sigh. 'He says he's found somebody else and that it's all over,' she said. 'I can't believe it . . . everything was so wonderful . . . '

Xinia listened, but only to be polite. She began a swift inspection of the cottage, climbing over books, skidding along oak window-ledges, sniffing at pot plants and greatly admiring the soft patchwork bedspread in Sally's bedroom. She was not yet entirely certain that Sally was a witch, but she thought she would hang around for a few days to make sure.

There were many things about Sally that were very witch-like. She had only to touch a small black box and the room was instantly full of discordant music like banshees let loose. She had a strange kind of crystal ball, square shaped, which again she had only to touch and people were captured on it, much smaller in size but actually in the room. Xinia often sat with her nose only inches away from the screen, mesmerised by a round black blob that whizzed about like a flying insect. Sometimes she would shoot out a paw to catch it, but she couldn't penetrate the magic.

'What are you doing?' Sally would laugh. 'Playing goalie?'

Sally seemed to spend a lot of time talking down a long, flexible cord, which, although clever, appeared pretty pointless to Xinia. She did not have a cauldron, but there was a grey pot she often put on the cooker which hissed ferociously in the most alarming manner.

What almost convinced Xinia that Sally was a witch was the discovery that Sally sometimes took off her hair. Xinia nearly jumped out of her fur the first time she found Sally's hair sitting on a stand on the dressing-table with no Sally underneath it. She sniffed at the wig cautiously, patting it with a tentative paw. It was real all right. It was even curly, whereas Sally's other hair was straight. Xinia was most impressed.

Sally was pretty lonely, even for a witch. She never seemed to go to any covens to meet other witches. She did a lot of gardening and talking to herself and reading letters and experimenting with spells that she called cooking. But often she sat in the evening gloom of the little sitting room, not bothering to put on the lights.

'I'm going to be an old maid,' she said one night, hugging Xinia tightly. 'They'll call me Sally the Spinster.'

Xinia thought this a very odd remark to make, especially when there wasn't a single spinning wheel in the house. She made a quick reconnaissance of upstairs and downstairs to make sure that Sally hadn't sneaked one in, but there was nothing more mechanical than a bag of crochet which Sally wasn't making much headway with.

Sally didn't sleep much, but then witches don't need much sleep. She often wandered about the cottage in the small hours of the morning, coming into the kitchen to make herself some hot milk.

Xinia didn't really mind being woken up by the light being switched on. Any time was milk time. But she did think all that crying on the kitchen table was taking things a bit far. Witches didn't usually shed tears, but this one did and Xinia objected to being used as a superior sort of paper tissue to mop up the tears trickling down Sally's cheeks.

'I do miss him so. What am I going to do?' she sobbed into Xinia's fur. 'Whatever am I going to do? I can't go on like this . . . I can't work . . . I can't think . . . it's awful.'

Xinia did a quick lick to rearrange her damp fur and agreed wholeheartedly. It certainly couldn't go on like this. They were both losing their beauty sleep, and Sally hadn't cast a really good spell all the time she'd been there.

Xinia went for a long, thinking walk, snapping at dragonflies, chasing ants and terrorising the stone dwarf who fished all day long in their neighbour's goldfish pond.

Of course, what Sally needed was another man so that she would stop missing this other one and start knowing what she was going to do. But she would never meet another man staying in the cottage all day reading sad books and trying to find out where she'd gone wrong in her crochet.

Xinia only knew one man. She'd met him at those four farms she had lived on. She remembered the nice polished smell of his boots and the gentleness in his voice as he tended a sick cow or a mare in labour. She even knew his name – Gavin Jones. But mostly people called him 'the vet', whatever that meant.

She knew where to find him, too. He had a rambling red-brick house where people brought all their sick animals – dogs with hot noses wrapped in blankets, and fractious cats in baskets, spitting straw. Xinia took to sitting in the middle of a flowerbed outside the surgery, waiting for Gavin Jones to come out.

'Hello, thing,' he said quite kindly several times as he got into his estate car to start on his rounds.

One morning he came out talking to a plump woman who was carrying a bandaged poodle.

'You'd better keep him warm, and make sure your husband's workshop is locked in future. I think life is getting more and more dangerous for our pets,' said Gavin Jones. Then he spotted Xinia among the French marigolds. 'Hello, thing,' he said.

Xinia gave him a long, cool stare, flicked her tail haughtily and then deliberately scratched up a geranium.

But what she had overheard was food for thought. Obviously being the vet had something to do with looking after pets in danger. Perhaps if she did something dangerous, then Gavin Jones would arrive at the cottage, meet Sally, and before you could say 'Mary Poppins' they'd be speeding down the M1 on a broomstick.

So that night Xinia made her bed in a box of old jam jars that Sally had been saving for the blackberry season. She trampled energetically, sliding and clattering jars about, making a great fuss and being terribly dangerous.

Sally fished her out and held the marmalade cat at arm's length. 'You great goof,' she laughed, her pretty dimples showing for the first time in days. 'You can't go to sleep on jam jars! Let me find you a nice new piece of blanket.'

The next day Xinia climbed on to the roof of the cottage, then leapt on to the chimney stack and pretended that she couldn't get down.

'Dinner time!' Sally shouted from the garden, banging a fork on a tin of cat food. Xinia tried to look pathetic and frightened. Then she did a little bit of pretending to jump and being overcome with terror at the brink.

'Oh, come on,' said Sally, exasperated. 'It's getting cold out here. I won't let you watch any telly!' she threatened.

Xinia crouched down and prepared to sit it out, hurt that Sally could be so ungrateful. Still, witches were unpredictable. It wouldn't do to upset one. She didn't want to be turned into a toad.

About half-past ten, Xinia picked her way down in the dark and pushed open the kitchen door. Sally was mashing some sardines in a saucer.

'Did you enjoy the view?' Sally asked sweetly, putting the saucer down on the floor.

But she had been crying again, and although Xinia was starving, she could not help twining herself round Sally's ankles a few times.

'Oh, pussy,' Sally sighed. 'You don't know what being in love is like . . . ' and she ran out of the room, forgetting to give Xinia any milk.

Xinia sat there, licking her paws, her mouth as dry as old fish bones. She couldn't open the cupboard where the milk stood up by itself. She jumped on to the draining-board but there wasn't a drip of water to be seen.

She wandered into the pantry and leapt up on to the marble shelf, jumping awkwardly because she was stiff from sitting on the roof all day. Normally she would never have knocked anything over, but something new was there – some contraption of tubes and funnels. Sally edited cookery books for a living and all sorts of strange things were always going on.

The contraption crashed to the ground, shattered, and a pale liquid spread all over the floor. Water, thought Xinia joyously. She leaped down and began to lap it up. Well, it wasn't quite water, but beggars couldn't be choosers. She drank her fill, but soon began to feel quite odd. Something was happening to the kitchen walls . . . perhaps Sally was doing a twirly spell?

Her head was muzzy and her legs felt as if they did not belong to her. Xinia looked down carefully and was relieved to see that they were still joined on. But what . . . on earth . . . was happening?

She staggered round the kitchen, suddenly quite merry

and happy. Of course, being such a young witch, Sally couldn't be expected to get everything right the first time, but still she was trying and that was a hopeful sign.

She was vaguely aware of Sally coming into the kitchen, all floating and misty in a white nightgown. Really this was getting better all the time. Levitation now.

'Whatever's the matter?' she heard Sally exclaim. Then Sally was talking in the hall. 'Hello? Hello? This is Sally Jenkins, six Elm Cottages. I'm so sorry to call you out so late, but I'm terribly worried about my cat. She's staggering about in the most unnatural manner . . . thank you very much.'

Xinia was clambering unsteadily up the stairs – or was she coming down the stairs? – when Gavin Jones arrived at the cottage. Sally opened the door to him, a large shawl wrapped round her shoulders, her amber hair clouding her pale face. He looked uncertainly at the vision of white and gold in the doorway, and coughed. 'Miss Jenkins?'

'I think she's drunk,' said Sally.

'You've got a sloshed cat?' he asked, wondering if he was dreaming.

'Please come in and have a look at her.'

'What was it? A drop of mother's ruin?' asked Gavin.

'No, my elderflower wine. It's been fermenting in the larder and she must have knocked it over and drunk some . . . '

'Ah . . . the raw stuff. Elderflower, eh? Can have quite a kick,' he said pleasantly.

Xinia saw two Gavin Joneses coming towards her. She didn't much mind which one picked her up. He held her very gently and stroked her in an understanding way.

'I think it might be best if we just let her go away and sleep it off somewhere safe,' he said a little later.

When Xinia eventually woke up around midday, Gavin Jones was in the kitchen having a cup of coffee with Sally.

'Hello, here comes the patient,' said Gavin, going down on to one knee. 'How are you feeling this morning? A bit groggy?'

'Will she have a hangover?' Sally asked anxiously.

'I've really no idea,' said Gavin, his eyes twinkling.

'Perhaps we ought to put her in touch with Alcoholics Anonymous before she gets a taste for elderflower wine. But first, a little warm milk . . . '

After that, the nice looking young vet was always at the cottage, whether Xinia was thinking up dangerous exploits or not. He either popped in on his way to somewhere, or on his way back from somewhere. Sometimes Sally grabbed a coat and went with him which was very promising. In fact, soon she had stopped crying, and the pile of letters on her dressing table were gathering quite a dust.

'The office phoned today to see how I was,' said Sally one evening as they were strolling in the garden. 'I only took a month's leave and it's nearly up. I shall have to go back to my editorial chair before they give my job to someone else.'

'I shall miss you,' said Gavin quietly.

'I'll be back most weekends,' said Sally, apparently pretending that she had not heard him. 'It's not really that far from London.'

Xinia sat in a tree half listening. She couldn't understand why Sally had to go . . . there were plenty of chairs in the cottage. What was so special about this editorial one? Perhaps it had some kind of magic.

Xinia stood on a branch and arched her back. She supposed, reluctantly, that it was time to move on. She'd never been absolutely sure that Sally was a witch, anyway.

Having decided, Xinia left without further ado. She walked straight down the road, across the fields and began to climb the hilly country. Before darkness fell it began to rain, lightly at first but soon it developed into a steady downpour. Then, after a low far-off rumbling, the sky suddenly burst with a clap of overhead thunder; lightning flashed across the dark clouds with crazy fingers. Xinia thought at first it was Sally's doing, making a spectacular fuss. But how could it be? All the time she had lived at the cottage, Sally had never once been angry. No, it must be some other lot.

Xinia tried to find a dry spot to shelter until the storm was over, but the hours of steady rain had soaked everything. Eventually she gave up the hills and found a road to walk on; the ditches were running with rain, and even the road was covered with deep, slopping puddles. Xinia stopped and shook the drops off her paws fastidiously.

Suddenly she was blinded by the headlights coming towards her along the road. Her wits vanished and she froze, petrified, convinced that it was a she-wolf, eyes flaring, jaws ready to crunch her into oblivion . . . The car screeched to a halt within yards of her. Both doors were flung open and a man and a woman got out, running through the torrential rain.

Xinia found herself being scooped up and crushed against a wet raincoat. Sally cradled the bedraggled cat like a baby.

'Whatever are you doing out here in the wilds?' she cried in amazement. 'You're miles from home and absolutely soaked. You'll get lost wandering off like this.'

'And run over . . . sitting in the middle of the road to tidy up,' said Gavin. 'Let's get back into the car. We were going out to dinner, but I suppose we can hardly take a drowned cat with us.'

Suddenly he put his arms round Sally and kissed her, standing in the middle of the road in the pouring rain.

'Don't you realise I love you?' he said, almost roughly. 'You've bewitched me and I'm utterly under your spell. You're beautiful . . . a beautiful witch.'

Xinia, squashed between two raincoats, forgot her discomfort. So Sally *was* a witch after all, quite definitely a witch. Gavin Jones couldn't be wrong. He knew everything.

'Let's take this scruffy thing home first,' he went on tenderly, 'and then we must have a talk . . . a proper talk.'

Sally nodded, smiling. 'That's a good name for her,' she agreed. 'Scruffy.'

Xinia went completely limp. She practically died with mortification. Scruffy! She would never get used to it . . . never, never.

She closed her eyes, nursing her wounded pride, as she was carried back to the car. Sally wrapped her in a warm knitted scarf and settled her comfortably on her lap.

'I hope she won't be frightened of the car,' said Sally. 'I don't suppose she's been in one before.'

But Xinia wasn't frightened. She wasn't frightened of anything. Soon she sat up and took an interest in her new surroundings, fascinated by the rivulets of rain and the windscreen-wipers chasing them, and the dark countryside flashing by.

'I'll put the heater on,' said Gavin. Then he touched another switch and the air was filled with soft, melodic sound.

Xinia was most impressed. This must be some sort of updated version of a broomstick, she thought. Well, it was certainly an improvement on the old type. . . .

3 THE COMMUTER

When Great-Aunt Hannah died she left all her worldly possessions to her nephew, Philip Newton. These consisted of a small, wisteria-clad, red-brick house on the outskirts of a town tucked away among the few remaining heaths and hills of Surrey, a frighteningly-depleted bank balance and a very large broad-shouldered silver tabby called Darby.

'We're just like Darby and Joan,' she used to tell the cat as they took their daily walk together past the old water-mill. 'Just you and me left now, pussy. And dear Philip, of course, although we don't see much of him, do we? He's working somewhere in Senegal, West Africa . . . dear me, I do believe I've never even heard of the place . . . '

Neither had Darby, but it did not bother him too much. Great-Aunt Hannah always talked to him as if he were a person and the actual content of her conversation was not important. He always listened attentively and then curled himself round her arthritic ankles to show that he understood . . . even when he didn't.

He knew when Great-Aunt Hannah came back from the hospital that she was not going to live long. From that moment he barely left her side. He gave up hunting. His only excursions into the garden were brief but necessary. He made sure that she was never lonely, and at night took to sleeping at the foot of her bed.

'You're better than a hot-water bottle,' she used to say, but was more glad of the sound of his even breathing when she woke in the early hours and waited for the dawn light.

He was there when she died, watching her face with his fathomless green eyes. Afterwards he sat like a large grey shadow outside the door of her room and would not move.

'I'm right glad you've come at last,' said Mrs Bevins, the next door neighbour who had been taking care of the house and Darby till Philip's return from West Africa. 'I've been real worried. I've done my best but he seems to be pining badly for the old lady.'

Philip swung himself out of his two-seater sports car, a lanky brown man, his face bronzed by the tropical sun. He was overcome with gloom as the empty house brought back memories, and he turned and unloaded his golf-clubs, his back-pack and his typewriter before answering Mrs Bevins. All three items had travelled the world with him as he earned a living and made a reputation as a freelance journalist. Now an international magazine had offered him a staff post, and the sad, unexpected windfall of a house within commuting distance of London had made up Philip's mind. He had accepted the job and was due to start on Monday.

'Who's pining?' he asked, his mind a dozen years away. 'Who's this? Some friend of my aunt's . . . ?'

'Not exactly a friend, Mr Newton. It's Darby. You know, her cat.'

'Of course, Darby,' said Philip. 'But it's only natural that he should mourn for her. I expect they were close companions.'

'But I didn't know that cats . . . er . . . did that,' Mrs Bevins said awkwardly.

'There are many mysteries in this life,' said Philip. 'And cats are one of them.'

Despite the profundity of this statement, Philip did not know how to solve the problem of what to do with Darby. The cat had not eaten for days and his beautiful black and silver fur hung loosely on his large frame like an empty bag. He sat quite still, wrapped in melancholy.

'Hello, old chap,' said Philip, tentatively scratching the cat behind his ears. 'Missing Auntie, are you? But life has to go on. Try a little drop of milk. . . .'

But Darby sat staring into the distance, as still as the Egyptian Goddess Bast, only the occasional twitch of a whisker betraying that he even breathed.

'I don't know what to do with you,' said Philip, sitting back on his heels. 'I can't make you eat. Auntie would hate to see you like this – she would be most upset.'

An answer-phone recording told him that the local vet was on holiday and that emergency calls only should be referred to the next county. So Philip hunted through the shelves at the local library, and took a pile of cat books to the girl at the counter. She had a mass of light brown hair tied back with velvet ribbon and wore large owlish glasses.

'You like cats, then,' she commented as she date-stamped the books and filed away Great-Aunt Hannah's tickets.

'I have inherited a depressed cat,' said Philip.

'I hope you'll find something that will help,' she said with a sweet smile before turning to the next borrower.

Philip put the books on his kitchen table and sorted through the indices for all references to 'Cats, sick.' After reading harrowing descriptions of infectious enteritis, abscesses, bites, worms and ear trouble, Philip found a paragraph which seemed to have some bearing on Darby's present condition.

'Nursing is very important because sick cats give up easily. They must not be left alone. They should be visited frequently and talked to cheerfully . . . tempt with tiny morsels of favourite food . . . ' Philip read aloud. Tempting with tiny morsels was not exactly how Philip had planned to spend his first weekend back in England, but he would give it a try, for Great-Aunt Hannah's sake. But what was Darby's favourite food, he wondered?

Philip assembled a tray and went to join Darby in his silent vigil outside her door. If Darby did not like any of the selection from Great-Aunt Hannah's larder, then Philip could see himself with a very odd menu for supper.

'OK buster, here we go,' said Philip, twisting the opener on a slim, flat tin. 'The first item for your delectation is A for anchovies . . . now what do you think of these?'

Not much apparently. Darby regarded Philip's offering with apathy. With an air of polite indifference he also refused to look at bread and butter, biscuits, crab and corned beef, dripping, egg, fishpaste, gravy, ham, ice cream, jelly, kipper fillets and a slice of liver sausage. Neither did he show any interest in the proprietary brands of cat food waved under his nose.

'Whatever am I going to do with you?' sighed Philip, forgetting to sound cheerful. It was already dusk and a hundred small tasks were waiting to be done. Still Philip persevered. He unscrewed a small sticky jar and held out a teaspoonful of malt extract with cod liver oil.

Darby's nose twitched. His memory went into reverse and, as if re-enacting an old dream, he sat back on his haunches and gracefully rose into a begging position. His paws captured Philip's wrist lightly and a rough tongue came out to lick at the thick brown goo. At that instant Philip remembered it was Darby's party trick. Great-Aunt had taught the cat to beg, but the contents of the spoon with which she rewarded him had always been a closely kept secret.

'So malt and cod liver oil is your weakness,' said Philip with some relief. 'But it's hardly a balanced diet, Darby.'

Darby licked the spoon clean and sat back. There was a gleam in his eyes as he turned to the tray of food. He was going through an emotional struggle, torn between loyalty to Great-Aunt Hannah and this new man to whom she had obviously entrusted the secret of his party trick. That must mean he was someone special, in which case a transference of allegiance might be the wish of his dear mistress . . .

Once having made up his mind, Darby was practical as well as loyal. He knew that crab would not come his way often, so obligingly finished it up along with a few other items so that Philip would not have to eat a supper of fishpaste hash. After a saucer of warm milk to wash it all down, Darby fell into an exhausted sleep right in the middle of the stairs.

Philip stepped carefully over his body. He felt sure that Darby would recover now. With that problem solved, he could concentrate on his career, building up a decent social life and putting down a few roots.

Philip and Darby settled into a routine. They did not see very much of each other as Philip left early in the morning to catch his commuter train, often working late or staying in London for a show or a party. But whatever time Philip returned home, Darby was always there in the front porch, under the wisteria, waiting to jump down and greet him with a friendly rub round the ankles.

Slowly Darby regained his former size and handsomeness. The black rings on his long tail showed up like glossy bracelets, the pale softness of his tummy like swansdown, the distinctive M mark on his forehead giving his big round face a faintly thoughtful expression. For some unknown reason, Darby continued to sleep half-way up the stairs, stretched right across the tread. It was a curious place to sleep, as if he were waiting to meet someone or needed to be aware of the exact movements of the household.

At the weekends Darby was content to sit and watch Philip tinkering with the car, or gardening, or painting the outside of the house. If Philip went to the golf course he would accompany him, sitting on the perimeter of the greens and waiting to see if the tantalising little white ball would roll his way.

'No, Darby. Don't touch,' Philip commanded as Darby crouched ready to spring. Darby obeyed reluctantly. Great Aunt Hannah had brought him up well.

'How's your depressed cat?' asked the girl at the library when Philip returned the books.

'The crisis is over,' said Philip. 'He's on the road to recovery.'

'I'm so glad. It must have been quite worrying. My sister's got a cat but he's never ill. In fact quite the reverse, he's a bundle of energy. He's a stray but nonetheless we would be really upset if anything happened to him. I'm afraid there's a sixty pence fine. The books are overdue.'

'Sorry,' said Philip, searching in his pockets for odd coins. 'I've been busy . . . working late rather a lot.'

'That's all right,' she smiled again. 'We need your

money. I see you are also interested in golf,' she commented, noticing the titles of his new batch of books.

'My recipe for keeping fit,' said Philip, wondering what she would look like with her hair loose and without those big glasses. He thought the effect would be strangely disturbing. She had an unworldly air that made one think of hazy summers long ago, half forgotten lines of poetry, a lingering melody . . .

It was not that Philip minded paying fines, but he found himself going to the library more frequently. He needed assistance on such topics as Flemish painters, orismology and the history of field sports, and Lois Brooks was quite willing to search for helpful books.

'What a lot of reading to get through,' said Lois, date-stamping Philip's weekend research. 'Don't you ever feel lonely?'

'On the contrary,' said Philip. 'As Martin Tupper wrote more than a hundred years ago: "A good book is the best of friends, the same today and for ever." And besides, I have my cat for company. He's a quiet, sedate sort and sits beside me for hours. He's probably getting on a bit.'

'Not at all like our cat!' said Lois. 'Ours never keeps still for a moment. He's always dashing about all over the place chasing his own tail, playing catch-me with the children, scampering up and down trees. A regular bundle of energy.'

It was when Philip stayed at home for a few days to write a difficult feature on the future of nuclear power that he noticed Darby had a habit of disappearing for long periods of time. Occasionally the cat made a lightning visit back to Philip's side at the typewriter, vanishing again before Philip could even offer some light refreshment.

But in the evening Darby returned for good, threw himself down near Philip's chair and immediately fell into a deep whisker-twitching nap before supper. He was still quite a small eater for such a large cat.

'Not going off your food again, are you, Darby?' Philip asked, offering the cat his daily teaspoonful of malt extract. Darby caught Philip's wrist in his usual gentle, well-mannered way and licked at his treat, a low, throaty purr starting up. 'You seem a bit worried about something these days . . . '

Darby was definitely in some sort of a state. When Philip began his writing each morning, Darby would hover, padding around, watching Philip with some puzzlement. Then he would suddenly leap out of a window and disappear for half the day. This happened every morning, but as soon as Philip returned to commuting to London, the tension in Darby vanished. He became the relaxed cat he had been before, and his welcome home to Philip in the evening was genuine and touchingly reliable.

'I'm blessed how you know what time I'm coming home,' said Philip late one night. It was nearing midnight and he had come off the last, empty, bleakly rattling train. The big tabby was waiting in his usual place under the wisteria. 'You must have been waiting hours. By the way, old chap, I've brought you a present.'

It was a narrow leather collar with 'Darby' engraved on the name plate. Philip fastened it round the cat's furry neck, making sure it was comfortable.

Philip stepped back to view the effect. 'It makes you look a bit like a dog,' said Philip, not quite sure.

Darby was perfectly willing to look a bit like a dog if that was what Philip wanted. He knew his own superiority. The comparison did not worry him. He knew that his fur was like silk, that his muscles rippled like those of a wild tiger, that he could leap over the moon, be as silent as a shadow, and was descended from the Caffre cat of Egypt. He knew all these things yet didn't possess an ounce of vanity.

The first thing Philip noticed about Darby the next evening was that an ordinary brown luggage label had been tied to his new collar. Philip lifted the cat and squinted at the dangling label, trying to read the writing on it.

'My name is Fuzzy-Bear. I lodge at Keats Cottage and my owners would like to know where I go at nights,' Philip read aloud. 'Fuzzy Bear?' he repeated. Darby pretended not to hear, struggling a little as if objecting to being held aloft like a parcel.

Before he left to catch the 8.17 am train the next morning Philip wrote out a fresh label and attached it to Darby's collar: 'FUZZY BEAR? What a ridiculous name! Great-Aunt Hannah christened me Darby, and Darby I remain.'

He pushed the cat gently outside and locked the front door. Darby sat on the step, totally unconcerned, and began to wash his ears. A fresh breeze scurried through the branches, ruffling his fur, making him look bigger than ever.

Commuting doth not always run smoothly, as Philip was to discover that day. The derailment of a goods train outside Clapham Junction threw the whole region into chaos. He only managed to get home by leaving the office early, queuing for a series of buses and then hitching a lift for the last few miles. The driver dropped him at the end of the leafy lane by the now-deserted station.

The wind was still blustery as Philip walked along the lane, his coat collar turned up against the chill, feeling thoroughly disconcerted and out of humour. Travelling to London was just about bearable when everything went right, but at this moment he felt a surge of longing for the freedom of his back-pack and his wanderings through Africa under the blazing sun.

He could hear the voices of children laughing in one of the gardens that backed on to the lane. The sounds carried high and clear in the evening air. Several small figures in dungarees and anoraks were chasing a cat. It scrambled up a tree, danced tantalisingly along a branch, then hung from the furthermost end, for all the world like a striped monkey.

'Darby!' Philip shouted, astonished.

The cat froze, almost in mid-swing.

'Fuzzy-Bear,' called Lois Brooks, coming out of the cottage. She was no longer wearing her glasses and her hair was loose and blowing across her face. And she looked every bit as disturbing as Philip had imagined.

Darby looked from one to the other, and if a large tabby cat hanging from a tree can look embarrassed, then Darby looked embarrassed. He slithered a few inches, digging his claws into the bark, his long tail dangling like a rope.

'So this is your lodger,' said Philip.

'Who dosses down at your place,' said Lois. 'For the night.'

'And weekends.'

Lois nodded. 'Quite an arrangement.'

Darby knew they were talking about him. He was facing a dilemma. He had to decide what to do when he could not hold on to the branch for a moment longer. The children had disappeared indoors, bored once the adults appeared. There was no easy way out.

'A bundle of energy, eh?' Philip went on. 'Plays with the kids . . . dashes about all over the place.'

'Hardly the antics of a sedate, elderly cat,' said Lois demurely.

Darby could hang on no longer. He fell to the grass, picked himself up, shook the bits out of his fur, walked over towards Philip and Lois and sat down exactly halfway between them.

'Ah, a born diplomat,' said Lois.

'Part of Great-Aunt Hannah's training,' said Philip. 'It seems that while I have been commuting to London, Darby has also been commuting.'

'And it's easy to understand why,' said Lois, going down on her knees to rub Darby's nose. 'He was used to Great-Aunt Hannah at home for company, and when you went out all day he was lonely. So, very sensibly, he looked around for someone to spend the day with and walked into my sister's house. It also explains why he would suddenly disappear in the evenings. From here he could hear the trains coming into the station. I suppose when he saw you coming along the platform, he knew it was time to go home.'

'And raced ahead of me through the back gardens, to be sitting in my porch waiting for me,' Philip chuckled. 'And all this dashing about . . . '

'. . . is merely feline second childhood,' Lois finished for him.

There seemed to be no good reason to curb Darby's sensible arrangement, though now Darby could walk openly along to the station with Philip before going on to Keats Cottage for his second breakfast.

In the evening, Philip called to pick up his cat and somehow it seemed natural to stay and talk to Lois and her sister and the children.

Darby basked contentedly in the warmth and love of his two homes, watching with approval as a certain relationship developed. Quite soon he might not have to do so much commuting. It made it almost worth being called Fuzzy-Bear.

4 THE CAT FROM NEXT DOOR

It was so undignified and that's what really got Herbie about living with the ever-expanding Robinson family. Sometimes he felt he must have been delivered in a Christmas stocking, gift-wrapped, but far more durable than the other playthings.

He knew if he saw six-year-old Katy donning her nurse's outfit then he was due for a blanket bath, and that meant being swathed in towels and ignominiously anointed with water. It meant having his face and ears washed which he particularly detested, but for the sake of Katy's gentle crooning and cuddling, he put up with these atrocities.

Eight-year-old Jane had thought up a torture of a different kind. He suffered being dressed in a matinee jacket, long nightie and bootees with a satin-ribboned bonnet flattening his ears. He endured being ridden up and down the road in the basket on the front of her bicycle. This was far worse than being pushed in the pram, because at least in the pram he could take a nose dive down to the foot of the cover and leave only his tail showing, whipping the pillow.

But in the bicycle basket, he was exposed to public glare and comment. He could not even have a good scratch. At the first sign of a slackening of Jane's attention, he would leap out on to the pavement, fly through gardens and across the fields to a secret place where he would hide long enough to divest himself of the hated garments.

This went on until Jane ran out of baby clothes.

Thomas, two years her senior and lanky with it, had a habit of putting Herbie on the top of doors. Just why, Herbie did not have the slightest idea. One minute he would be curled up happily on some abandoned school blazer, then . . . whoops! He would find himself being born aloft by Thomas and deposited on the top edge of an open door, scratching and clawing to gain a balance. Once there he could remain lying along the edge with complete indifference until rescued by some adult Robinson.

Herbie was a Bi-coloured Shorthair. He could be described as a black cat with white splodges or a white cat with black splodges. It depended on the angle of viewing which colour was predominant. He had a small, alert face with intelligent eyes and neat ears. No one was quite sure of his age. He came sort of before Katy and after Jane. His birthday was celebrated on the date of the Battle of Waterloo, 18 June, when he was encouraged in vain to blow out the candles on a nice piece of cod fillet and all day it was cream, cream, cream in his saucer.

He ate well with the Robinsons. They were always saying he was the only cat in Great Britain who got meals on wheels. This was because Grandma Robinson was too old to have new teeth fitted, and anything she fancied but couldn't manage went into his bowl. Herbie was game to try anything from trifle to spaghetti bolognese. He was not fussy.

Herbie loved boxes. They were his all-consuming passion. He would get into any box, trying it out for size. He would investigate the depths of paper bags, plastic carriers, handbags, suitcases, typewriter lids . . . you name it, he would get into it.

When the crates arrived he was delighted and curious. But when he made a few tentative forays, there were immediate shrieks of 'Mind the china!' 'Off that linen!' 'Help, that one's full of glasses!' and eventually, 'Will somebody put Herbie out, *please?*'

So Herbie sat in the garden and watched. There were no blanket baths and rides on bicycles these days. Everyone was so busy. He did not quite understand what was going on.

One morning the Robinson family assembled outside with bags and parcels and he was being passed round for hugs and wet kisses. It was all very messy and he still did not understand what was happening. He hoped it didn't mean that he was going down the road. Several of his elderly friends had told him that hugs and wet kisses meant going down the road and not coming back.

So Herbie was quite relieved when it was evident that the Robinsons were not intending to put him in the car as well as all their family and the mountain of luggage. He rubbed his head against Katy's new ankle socks to show that he forgave her all the medical ministrations.

'We don't really want to leave him behind, but what else can we do?' said Mrs Robinson. 'One is always hearing about cats that walk back to their old homes and how could Herbie cope with all that ocean? We're so grateful for your kind offer.'

'Shall I have a new kitten in Australia?' asked the fickle Jane.

'Of course, darling.'

'Don't worry, Mrs Robinson, I'll look after Herbie for you,' said a new, sweet young voice. 'He'll be perfectly all right with us. I'm sure he'll soon get used to us and we'll take great care of him.'

Katy wept more water all over Herbie's ears. 'Goodbye, darling Herbie,' she whispered. 'I'll never forget you, never, never, never . . .'

It was very disturbing, and then amid a great deal of noise the Robinsons drove off, leaving Herbie and the sweet voiced young woman on the front lawn. He looked at her, wondering what was going to happen next. She was very young and quite tall. He hoped she was not going to put him on top of doors. She regarded him a little uncertainly, her fairish hair brushing her cheek like a breeze stirring a cobweb in the moonlight.

'Come along,' she said, trying to sound brisk. 'You live next door now.'

He did not move for two reasons. Firstly he did not know what next door meant, and secondly he was a mite worried about the door bit. Chrissie picked him up carefully and gave him a few little pats. 'Come along,' she said, again, more cheerfully. 'This way . . . '

The next door house was joined on to the Robinson's house and it was exactly the same, except that it was all the other way round. He discovered that Chrissie and Alan Marshall were newly-weds, that they lived in empty rooms and went out all day. It was very strange. Sometimes Herbie thought he had gone deaf.

It was an odd house. There was nothing to jump on, knock over, hide behind, sit on, scratch at, sniff at, trample on or investigate. Most of the time Herbie sat in the middle of the kitchen floor, polite and distant, grooming himself and slightly nauseated by the pervading smell of paint. He missed the Robinsons and all the noise and activity. He missed being talked to and included as part of the family.

'Herbie doesn't seem very happy,' said Chrissie for the hundredth time. 'He behaves like a visitor.'

'Perhaps we ought to show him round,' Alan suggested. 'That might make him feel at home.'

'It's very difficult when you've never had a cat before,' said Chrissie. 'I never know what to do.'

'Don't worry, darling. They are very independent creatures, aloof and stand-offish. It's probably just his way.'

Alan hoisted Herbie off the floor and carried him up the stairs. He flung open the first door with a flourish.

'Now, this is the spare room,' he announced, putting Herbie down on the lino. Herbie was amazed. It had been impossible to move in the Robinson's spare room when they had one. It had always looked like a central sorting depot for Oxfam. But this spare room was totally without interest . . . he prodded the two tennis rackets with some apprehension.

'Careful, old chap,' admonished Alan. He steered Herbie out of the spare room and into the next room. 'And this is our bedroom. We sleep here,' he added unnecessarily.

Herbie made a flying leap on to the rose-patterned duvet. It sank most satisfyingly, but before he had even done half a turn, Chrissie had whisked him off again.

'Sorry,' she said. 'Not on the bed.'

He was not allowed on the two armchairs either, or on the draining board, or in Chrissie's shopping basket, or in the linen cupboard or under the television set. So he took to staying in the middle of the kitchen floor, quiet and withdrawn, sometimes pretending to be asleep or watching a bee buzzing against a window-pane trying to get in.

The garden was immaculate and everything was in measured rows. Herbie learned to tread carefully. He found it hard to stalk tigers in an organised jungle of Tom Thumb lettuces, or scare birds who were already wary of all the flapping labels.

The best spot was the greenhouse, baking warm and out of the draught. But Alan was growing grass in trays and kept shutting Herbie out.

'Shoo . . . mind the cuttings. Off my seedlings, old boy.'

Herbie lost weight despite the fact that the Marshalls were kind to him and fed him. But Herbie's heart began to fail when he saw Chrissie reaching yet again for the tin opener. He longed for a bit of fruit cake and some cold cocoa.

He made one visit to the Robinson's old house but never again. A horrible sloppy dog with ears hanging down like soup plates had moved in. Herbie shuddered and kept to his side of the fence.

Sometimes he sat on the pavement outside and watched people go by on bicycles and in cars. One young woman with red-streaked hair always stopped and stroked him, knowing the special place under his chin just above where his purr started.

Sometimes he followed children along the road, but he was afraid to go too far. He was less trusting than he used to be. Especially after the field-mouse episode. He had only meant it as a gift for Chrissie. It was such a tiny thing and was paralysed with terror. Yet Chrissie had shrieked as if being attacked by a rampaging bull elephant. Herbie simply did not understand her and brought no more gifts.

The situation improved somewhat when Chrissie stopped going out every day. She started to sing around the house and that was rather nice. However, although she sat around quite a lot Herbie was never invited on to her lap. He now learned that he must not sit on her sewing or try to get into her knitting bag. The tennis rackets were moved into the back of the broom cupboard and some furniture was delivered for the spare room. Alan began hammering in the evenings and Herbie watched the shelves going up with interest.

'Off you come, Herbie. They won't take your weight,' said Alan, lifting him down.

'He's just testing,' said Chrissie with new perception.

Alan kissed her tenderly.

'Funny girl,' he said, ruffling her hair.

One day a new smell arrived in the house. Herbie recognised it immediately. It was the thin, sweet smell of milk. Something stirred and breathed in the pram parked in the hallway, and made small mewing sounds.

Herbie pricked up his ears. Surely it was not another cat? He stood up on his back legs and peered in, but the mesh of the cat-net obscured whatever lay under the mound of blankets.

'Say hello to Timmy,' said Chrissie, picking Herbie up with a growing confidence. It was the first time that Herbie had felt safe and not about to be dropped. He trembled slightly with a small rush of emotion.

Now the improvements began to accelerate at a rate of knots. Chrissie left things on the floor and was far too busy to notice if Herbie sat on them. All sorts of boxes and pails and bins began to appear in the kitchen.

'What on earth shall I do with this cereal?' Chrissie wailed one breakfast time. 'Timmy won't touch it.'

'Give it to the cat,' said Alan.

Baby cereal! One of Herbie's favourites. His rough little tongue could hardly lap it up for purring. Then at teatime it was marmite soldiers dropped all over the floor in various stages of squashed disintegration.

'Oh, you are a messy baby,' said Chrissie, hurrying to clear up, but Herbie was there before her. It seemed like years since he'd had a marmite soldier.

The baby soon began to crawl and then there wasn't a thing Chrissie could do about life at floor level. It became a glorious landscape of wooden bricks, round-eyed ducks, chewed crusts, lost shoes, sticky spoons and a fat yellow teddy bear who kept falling over. Herbie sat amid the chaos, keeping an eye on the baby, keeping his claws sheathed and never getting in the way. He was still rather like a visitor.

One afternoon Chrissie was sewing while her baby played on the floor with some empty cotton reels. Herbie was sunning himself by the window when through half an eye he saw the baby reaching up towards the flex of a reading lamp.

No one really knew whether he remembered the occasion when Katy Robinson did the same thing and brought the whole contraption crashing down on her head, but in a split second Herbie leaped off the windowsill and sent the baby flying back on his bottom on the carpet. The baby howled in surprise and one chubby fist shot out and grabbed at Herbie's long waving tail.

It hurt. It hurt very much. Herbie was almost transfixed with pain. He dug his claws into the carpet.

Then Chrissie was down on her knees, scolding the baby, hugging Herbie. Or was it hugging the baby and scolding Herbie? It did not really matter for Herbie's heart was leaping up into a joyful rumble of happiness.

For in that moment Herbie had looked into Timmy's eyes, and had seen a faint but unmistakable vision of blanket baths, and bicycle rides and door tops, and perhaps even worse. But it meant Herbie had a home. The move was complete. Next door had become home. At last.

5 ESMERALDA

Esmeralda lay lazily in the garden soaking up the warm sun. She yawned daintily, showing her small pink tongue.

Then she stretched out her limbs and abandoned herself to sun-worship. A small fly buzzed nearby but Esmeralda did not twitch a whisker. The heat was glorious and nothing bothered her.

Esmeralda was a large long-haired marmalade cat. The colours of her fur ranged from the rich rust of autumn leaves to pale top-of-the-milk cream. Her eyes were almond-shaped pieces of glinting amber that could change from pleading, bewitching or being scornful in seconds.

Esmeralda lived with Joelle. Joelle Martin was a very up-and-coming ballerina with the New London Ballet Company. She was slim and beautiful and even in jeans she walked like floating thistledown. All her movements flowed like liquid, and Esmeralda, who was a great lover of beauty, would often watch Joelle just for pleasure.

Sometimes Esmeralda would settle herself on Joelle's bed and watch her mistress brushing her long raven hair, or drawing on those incredible gossamer tights. Or she would sit on the windowsill, still watching, as Joelle moved round the kitchen, reaching up to put away the blue-spotted china in the cabinets.

There were times when Joelle and Esmeralda seemed strangely akin to each other. Often Joelle stretched like a cat, and Esmeralda was all ballerina when she twirled on her toes to pat a fluttering butterfly, or ran lightly along the top of the garden wall.

They lived in a tiny converted cottage on the outskirts of Westerham – for Esmeralda's sake.

'I couldn't bear to have Esmeralda shut up all day in a flat,' said Joelle when she told her friends of her move.

So Joelle travelled every day to London by train. Night after night she returned home very late from the theatre on the last train, carrying her weary body like a dispirited faun. She often slept late into the morning, and Esmeralda would find it necessary to jump on to her bed and pat her mistress's face so that she would wake up and provide breakfast.

'You're better than any alarm clock,' murmured Joelle sleepily, throwing a bare arm over the fluffy cat. Esmeralda was flattered but still hungry enough to nudge her mistress's ear.

'All right, all right, bully-puss. I'm getting up . . . '

Esmeralda and Joelle agreed on almost everything. They agreed on whether to go out or stay in, whether to eat or not eat, whether to clean or not clean, whether to garden or not garden. It was all most amicable. They agreed on mostly everything, that is, except about men.

Esmeralda did not like men. Men totally, full stop. On the whole they had big feet and she did not like big feet. They had loud voices, clumsy ways, smelt different and were a race apart. A few she would tolerate – at a distance – but the rest she disliked wholeheartedly.

But Joelle, being both beautiful and sweet-natured, gathered men-friends in droves. They descended on the cottage in cars, on motorbikes, on mopeds, or more rarely by train and then by foot.

Suede Shoes was a train person. Esmeralda tolerated Suede Shoes because he stroked her gently and did not disarrange her long fur. But she could never hear him approaching in his suede shoes and he often gave her a fright.

He too was a dancer. A choreographer in Joelle's company. He and Joelle would talk dancing for hours. Sometimes Joelle would float off into the garden and try new steps to music from the stereo, while the choreographer improvised and made suggestions. Esmeralda sat on a step and purred. It was all quite beautiful to watch from a distance, but his sudden flying leaps were very alarming. One sign of a leap and Esmeralda was off.

Suede Shoes did not like the journey from London. 'I don't know why you've buried yourself in the country, Joelle,' he would say in his thin, high voice. 'It makes it so difficult to come and see you at weekends. The train service is abysmal.'

Joelle would smile at him and try to explain.

'Esmeralda likes it here, and so do I. It's so peaceful.'

Grey Pin-Stripe was altogether a different matter. He came in a flashy car. He wore shiny black shoes, and fastidiously picked off all the long hairs that Esmeralda left on his turn-ups. 'Shoo . . . shoo . . . scat,' he would say sharply when Joelle was out of hearing.

Esmeralda was a naturally polite cat and only went to greet visitors, male or female, out of good manners. But when she got to know the sound of Grey Pin-Stripe's car, she sat on the wall with her back to him.

Once he left his overcoat on the old rocking chair in the hall. Esmeralda trampled happily all over it and made a bed right in the middle. After that, he was always careful to hang up his coat.

Grey Pin-Stripe was a banker and he bought beautiful and expensive presents for Joelle. His car was low, sleek and powerful. In desperation to win Joelle's love, he brought Esmeralda a wicker travelling basket. It took her several weeks of chewing to demolish the edges, then she totally ignored it.

'Devil of a drive out here,' Grey Pin-Stripe complained for the hundredth time. 'That turning before the village is a real bottle-neck. And the traffic's nose to tail once you reach the outskirts of London. Heaven knows what time I'll get home tonight. And I've a heavy day tomorrow.'

Joelle picked up Esmeralda and hid her amusement in the tawny fur. 'Esmeralda and I hardly hear the traffic from our little garden,' she said.

But just now, with the sun warming her deliciously,

Esmeralda was not thinking about Joelle's various men friends. She was dozing, half watching an ant running about on a smooth stone . . .

She heard a car slow down and stop at their gate. It was a small, noisy car and one she had not heard before. She decided it was too hot to go and see who it was. She did open one amber eye when a tall young man walked down the garden path. He had the reddest hair she had ever seen – Esmeralda felt quite a pale ginger in comparison. He had a kind brown face and eyes as blue as the sky. He stooped a little as though he were weary or the small car had left him with cramp.

Suddenly Esmeralda found herself lifted into the air. She struggled frantically, waving her velvet paws like windmills.

'Why, hello gorgeous,' said a deep, friendly voice. 'I didn't know there were two beauties in the family.'

Esmeralda stopped waving and stared at him, one paw suspended in mid-air. She rather liked being thought gorgeous. Joelle came out of the back door. She had on her old faded jeans and a loose sweater, but even in those clothes she walked like a dancer. She smiled hesitantly at the stranger holding her cat, then her smile warmed as she recognised him.

'Hello. You're the doctor who came and looked at my ankle last night, aren't you?'

'That's right. I was wondering how my patient was this morning,' he said, stroking Esmeralda behind the ears. 'I hope you don't mind my coming out here to your home. The stage doorman gave me your address. Only, of course, when I explained my medical interest,' he added quickly.

'It's very kind of you to bother. It's a long way.'

'It's not far really. Besides, a spin in the countryside is rather refreshing after night duty.'

Both Joelle and Esmeralda looked at the young man with red hair again. He was the first man not to mind the journey, they noted, even after a night's work.

'I hope you weren't taken away from anything important last night,' said Joelle quickly, a little alarmed by her thoughts. 'It was such a slight accident. I didn't really want them to go and fetch a doctor.'

'The hospital is only a few doors away from the theatre so it was no trouble to come and see what was the matter. You managed to get home all right?'

'Oh yes, it was really a lot of fuss about nothing.'

'No injury, however slight, is a fuss about nothing. Especially for a dancer.'

Joelle could not believe her ears. She asked him to stay for some coffee. While she went indoors to put on the percolator, the young man carefully put Esmeralda down on the spot where he had first found her. 'Just go on promoting that tan of yours, my beautiful,' he said.

After that, Esmeralda saw quite a lot of the young man with red hair. Every time he had a day off from the hospital he came down to the cottage and made himself useful. He trimmed the hedge and painted all the window frames bright yellow. When autumn came he swept up the leaves and carted them to the rubbish dump in a wheelbarrow, with Esmeralda hitching a ride on top. But when he chopped wood for the open fire, she kept to a safe distance, eyeing the flying chips with caution.

Joelle cooked him nourishing meals and he began to look less pale and tired. She was glad to see the change in him.

Suede Shoes still came down, and so did Grey Pin-Stripe, but Joelle never looked happier than when she was with the young man with red hair.

To Suede Shoes, she was always foremost a dancer. He never allowed her to forget that or her career. To Grey Pin-Stripe, she was a famous name it was flattering to be seen with. Neither of them saw her as a real person. But when the young doctor came, she was able to forget her career and her fame. He saw her as a shy, vulnerable person, beautiful and talented and way out of his reach.

Esmeralda knew that he wanted to marry Joelle. He often told her about it as she watched him working in the garden.

'You know, Esmeralda,' he confided in her one day. 'I'm wishing for a bright star, a star so bright that I haven't the nerve to pluck it from the sky.'

Esmeralda wound herself round his ankles to comfort

him. She knew he was not very rich. Anyone could tell that from his shaky old car; and Esmeralda, from her viewpoint, could see that his nicely-polished brown shoes had been mended many times and the turn-ups of his good tweed, comfortable suit were showing signs of age.

Red was determined to take Joelle to his hospital ball. He bought the tickets, cleaned his car, sent Joelle a single camellia and arrived at eight o'clock looking incredibly handsome in a hired dinner jacket.

'I'm almost ready, Red,' Joelle called from her bedroom.

Of course his name was Red. Esmeralda had guessed that all along. It had come as no surprise when Joelle had whispered that his name was Dr Red Carter.

Red bent down to say hello to Esmeralda. 'I can't pick you up this evening, my beauty. You'd just ruin this suit, I'm afraid.'

Then Joelle swirled out of her room, clouded in midnight blue chiffon, with her dark hair gleaming. On the single diamond-studded strap of her dress she had pinned the camellia.

'Oh Joelle,' Red murmured, unable to take his eyes off her.

They went off into the night, leaving Esmeralda in the kitchen like Cinderella.

When they returned in the early hours of the morning, the air was warm with love. Theirs was a secret happiness and their hands touched as they moved about the room, drawing the curtains, switching on the electric fire, putting a romantic record on the stereo.

Then, as the gentle sounds floated through the room they were drawn into each other's arms. Their lips met in a kiss that lifted them to the stars. Suddenly Joelle broke away and ran to the french windows. She flung them open and ran on to the lawn, the folds of her blue chiffon dress streaming behind her. She danced like a fairy on the grass, light and beautiful, till she flew back to Red's arms and his words of love.

However, the next morning Esmeralda found her mistress weeping into her pillow, her hair tangled and wet.

'I've told him I can't marry him, Esmeralda. I can't, I really can't,' she cried into the cat's long fur. 'I can't give up my career, my dancing, just to be a doctor's wife. And it would mean leaving London when he becomes a GP. No . . . I just couldn't . . . it's too much to ask . . .'

Esmeralda jumped on to the windowsill and licked her fur back into place as her mistress went on crying. For many days Joelle wore a tired, lost look on her face, and Esmeralda knew she was not sleeping for Joelle often crept into the kitchen in the small hours to make a warm drink of milk.

Dr Red Carter came no more to the cottage, the garden drifted into neglect, and Esmeralda missed his friendly company. Every time she heard a noisy car, the cat went flying down the path to meet him. But she was always mistaken and would arch her back as the offending vehicle went by.

Joelle became more and more absent-minded and withdrawn. Four times she ran out of cat food, and Esmeralda's daily brush and comb stopped being fun because Joelle was so quiet and unhappy. Once she locked up at bedtime without letting Esmeralda in and the cat spent a lonely night under a hedge.

Esmeralda watched her mistress with narrowing eyes. It was these men who had brought unhappiness to Joelle and discomfort to Esmeralda's orderly life.

One day, as Esmeralda lay sprawled on the path in her favourite spot, contemplating the busy fussing of a colony of ants, she decided that Joelle needed something to rouse her from her unhappiness. Some kind of shock. Dried cat snacks were no substitute for a nice piece of fresh coley.

She stood up slowly and stretched, her fur prickling with sensuous delight as her limbs quivered and relaxed. She stalked down to the end of the garden, eyeing the different trees with apparent unconcern.

Joelle had risen late, heavy-eyed and listless. She was brushing her hair by the window when she first became aware of a plaintive miaowing. She put on her blue dressing-gown and ran out into the garden. High up on the topmost branch of a spindly ash tree she could see a small blob of orange fur.

'Esmeralda!'

The cat answered with a faint miaow. Her fluffy tail swung erratically. A breeze moved the slender branch and Esmeralda dug her claws into her precarious perch. She had climbed higher than she had intended.

'Oh poor Esmeralda . . . don't be frightened. Try and climb down. Come on, Esmeralda. Puss, puss, puss . . . fish, fish, fish . . . '

Joelle called and coaxed but Esmeralda clung to her swaying branch like a sailor to rigging in a storm. She would have to get help, thought Joelle desperately. As she ran indoors to the telephone, Esmeralda watched her disappearing figure with hope.

Joelle dialled the number of the theatre. It was some minutes before Suede Shoes came to the phone.

'My dear Joelle, I'm in the middle of a rehearsal,' he scolded gently. 'Do be brief. You know how I hate to be disturbed. It simply ruins my emotional flow. Esmeralda? Up a tree? Well, I don't see what I can do about it. Now, now, don't take it like that, Joelle, of course I'm fond of Esmeralda . . . Try waving a piece of fish tied to a broomstick. Surely you're not expecting me to climb up after her?' His voice rose to a higher pitch. 'Why, I might fall!'

Joelle slammed down the receiver, trembling with disgust. The man was a coward.

She dialled a city number and after speaking to two secretaries she eventually reached the great executive himself.

'Joelle? How nice to hear from you,' said Grey Pin-Stripe, full of his usual charm. 'I've been meaning to give you a ring ever since I got back from Zurich. How are things, darling?'

When Joelle explained Esmeralda's plight, Grey Pin-Stripe exploded.

'Up a tree? Do you mean to say that you've phoned me at my office to tell me that your idiotic cat is marooned up a tree? How do you know it's marooned? Perhaps it likes being there. Look here, my dear Joelle, I'm devoted to you. You are an exquisite woman, but I have a board meeting in a quarter of an hour and my time is valuable. Surely you are not expecting me to come down and rescue your feline companion myself?'

Joelle began to weep quietly.

'Now, now, don't take it so badly. Here's what I'll do. I'll phone the fire brigade. They'll rescue your perishing cat in a jiffy.'

'Esmeralda's not a perishing cat,' Joelle retorted. 'And don't bother to ring the fire brigade. You might waste two minutes of your precious time. I'll ring them myself. Goodbye!'

She rang them immediately and was told that the tender was already out but that the officers would be given the message when they returned.

Slowly she dialled a fourth number. She did not know what she would say, or what to expect, so it was with relief that she heard that they were unable to contact him. Dr Carter was busy, would she leave a message? Joelle sighed. There was nothing she could say. Red's job really was important.

'No, thank you. There's no message.'

An hour later the fire brigade arrived. Joelle was still wandering round the garden distractedly in her dressing-gown, coaxing and pleading with the errant Esmeralda. The fireman began to unload their equipment in the lane.

'Don't worry, miss. We'll soon have her down.'

The young fireman gave a cheerful grin and began to climb the extending ladder that stretched up into the highest branches of the tree.

'Come along, Ginger,' he called to Esmeralda. 'Nice pussy.'

The nice pussy arched her back like an outraged porcupine and hissed.

'Now then, Ginger-nob, I won't hurt you,' he coaxed.

Every one of Esmeralda's hairs stiffened at the insult. Ginger, Ginger-nob indeed! She backed further out of reach along the swaying branch. As she eyed the fireman with distaste, Esmeralda heard a familiar noise coming along the lane. The car stopped at the gate and Red Carter hurried down the garden path, going straight to Joelle.

'I came as quickly as I could,' he said. 'I knew there must be something wrong.'

'Oh Red, I didn't mean you to come. But I am glad, so very glad that you have.'

'I had to finish Casualty first, or I would have been here sooner.' His keen blue eyes swept over the scene, missing nothing from the soft flush on Joelle's cheeks, her wild-eyed desperation, to the waving fireman perched at the top of the ladder.

'I'd better go up there,' he said, taking off his coat. 'Esmeralda won't come down for a stranger.'

The fireman descended and wiped his brow. 'Coo, proper little tartar, that one. Mad as a hatter, spitting and hissing. You'll get more than a couple of scratches if you manage to get hold of her.'

'At least she knows me,' said Red, trying to sound confident. The rungs of the ladder stretched upwards into nothingness. In all his years of hospital work, he had never faced anything more terrifying. He hated heights and the thin, waving ladder only made it worse.

Red gritted his teeth and put his foot on the first rung. Slowly he forced himself to climb. His feet felt like lead and the palms of his hands were slippery with sweat. He did not dare look down, and suddenly his fear communicated itself to those watching down below.

Joelle ran to the foot of the tree. He did not look at all safe. She realised how much he meant to her, and always had. 'Come back,' she shouted. 'Please, Red, come down. I can't stand it. You'll get hurt. Please, darling . . . '

Esmeralda peered out between the leaves. Her small, crinkled face looked worried. Suddenly she knew what she must do.

With a tremendous leap, she left her high perch and sank her claws into a lower, sturdier branch. Then, sliding, scratching, clawing wildly at anything within grasp, she slithered down the tree, landing at Joelle's feet amid a shower of leaves and twigs. But before Joelle could pick her up, she was off like a bullet across the garden, disappearing through the hedge and away to the meadows.

'Well, I'm blowed,' said the fireman. 'These damned cats . . . '

Shakily Red descended to earth. Joelle went up to him and put her arms around him.

Not far away, Esmeralda sat under a hawthorn, licking her disarranged fur into place. Now perhaps she would have some peace at home. And with that comforting thought she swatted at a fly and started to purr rapturously.

6 THIS MAN IS MINE

She had been living with him now for almost a year. The time had flown and neither of them had really noticed the months passing. He was a man worth loving, a man with his head among the stars, dreaming and thinking and plucking ideas out of the bright dark night with long, slender fingers. He was an author, writing under the name of Graham Marsh, but she did not know if this was his real name.

They lived in quiet, rural happiness with never a quarrel to mar the peaceful days in that small Devonshire cottage. He asked nothing more of her than that she should always be there. And so she was, ready to greet him on his return from London, or from the nearby market town – waiting to welcome him home.

He asked that she should be quiet and undemanding when he was writing, but that she should be ready with affection during the long evenings. The perfect lover. And how she loved him on those evenings, waiting for the moment when he would push aside his papers and smile at her. Then she would come into his arms, and his soft words of love were music to her ears.

She rarely left the cottage, partly because she was still a little nervous of the outside world. He had given her a home when she was most lonely and afraid. He had offered her a haven.

She did not like travelling in his car because it made her feel sick, nor did she like fishing with him in his little boat because she was afraid of the dark blue sea. So she stayed at home, happy to wander round the little cottage and its sunny, flower-filled garden.

But she also liked it when they walked together into the surrounding countryside. Sometimes his long legs tired her and then, if there was a field with poppies and butterflies, she would sit and daydream and wait for him to return.

There was no doubt that Graham adored her. 'You have beautiful eyes, my love,' he would say, staring into their amber-flecked depths as if seeking some truth there. Then he would run his hands over her face and rest his cheek against the softness of her neck.

And she loved him till sometimes she thought her heart would burst, and she just had to go over to him where he sat at his desk and touch his sleeve or make some small gesture of love. But when he was working, he had little time or thought for her.

'Go away, Susy,' he would say, not unkindly. 'Leave me alone, there's a good girl.'

She did not sleep with him but had her own bed in another room. Once she had come to him in the middle of a cold, wintry night when the temperature had fallen and frost was biting the air with icy needles. She had stood in the doorway of his bedroom. But he had been angry with her and had escorted her back to her own bed. She had heard his door shut firmly and had not been able to understand his harshness.

Then one day – a day in early spring – when the garden was full of nodding daffodils and the long green pods of unopened tulips, Graham came home early from seeing his publishers in London. He stood in the porch and Susy ran to him, wanting him to take her into his arms as he always did. But today he stepped back, and she saw that his arms were full. In them he held a small bundle wrapped in a blanket.

Susy faltered in her approach and looked up at him questioningly.

'I've brought a baby home for you, Susy,' he said softly. 'A little baby for you to look after.'

He turned so that she could see what was in the blanket,

and the small blue eyes that regarded her were startlingly clear and unafraid.

'This baby has no home,' he added, 'and you and I are going to look after the poor little mite.'

Susy saw the baby look up at him with adoring eyes, and anger began to smoulder in her heart. He was her man. He belonged to her, and no one else. She did not want to share him with anyone – not even a baby.

She backed away sullenly, not even welcoming him as she usually did, then suddenly it was all too much and she turned and ran upstairs, her heart turning over and over in a turmoil of jealousy and love for him.

'Oh, come on, Susy. Come downstairs and don't be such a silly girl,' he called out after her.

But she did not answer, nor did she come downstairs. She heard him talking to the baby then preparing its food in the kitchen, and she began to hate it. Oh, why did he have to do this to them, she cried to herself, when they had always been so happy together?

Hours later, feeling hungry and desolate, she crept downstairs. The door to his study was ajar. She stood silently in the shadows and saw that he was holding the baby on his lap and it was sleepy with milk. His papers lay on his desk, untouched.

Susy fled out into the garden, not caring where she went, running wildly through the flowers, shaking with a storm of rage. She ran to her favourite tree, a lilac, and climbed a little way, sitting and plotting against this newcomer. She heard Graham come to the door and call her name, but she took no notice. She did not return to the cottage until she saw the lights go out, then she trod softly into the kitchen.

She was very hungry by now, but was almost too angry to eat or drink anything. It would have choked her.

She wandered round quietly, looking for the baby. Where was it? She stood outside the door to his bedroom and her senses quickened. The baby was in his room! She could hear its small movements. She crept away, cowed and beaten, but loving him still despite the misery in her heart.

So the baby came to live with them, and they were three.

It was female and for the time being its name was just Baby. Susy refused to look after her, and once Graham had accepted her decision, he was not angry any more but simply laughed and teased her about it.

'Why, Susy, I do believe you're jealous!' he would say. 'Fancy being jealous of a scrawny little mite with a screwed up face, when you are beautiful and I love you.'

But Susy was still and unrelenting in his arms. It was not easy to forgive him.

So Graham took care of the baby and saw to her small needs. He loved to encourage her unsteady efforts to walk and gave her a soft, woolly ball to play with. When she was tired, he carried her in his arms, while Susy sat and watched from a distance, hatred in her narrowed eyes.

Now in the evenings it was the baby he cuddled on his lap, and Susy slunk sadly away for she could not bear the sight of them together. However, if he wanted to smoke his pipe, he put Baby down, frightened that hot ash might fall on her. It was then that Susy crept back into his arms, burying her face against his neck, trying to ignore the swirling puffs of smoke from his pipe for the sake of being with him again.

'Just like old times, Susy,' he would say to her, and she would soften with love for him all over again.

One day he had to go up to London, and he asked her to look after the baby. He stood in the doorway, tall and handsome in his city suit and polished shoes.

'Now will you be a sweetheart and take care of Baby for me?' he asked. He turned her face so that she had to look straight at him. 'Can I trust you?' he added seriously. Susy turned away so that he could not see her eyes, and in answer she went over to the baby and began to wash her half-heartedly.

He sighed with relief. 'That's a good girl. I'll be home tomorrow, but there's plenty of food for you both.'

Susy waited until she heard his car going down the lane, then she stopped washing the baby and shook her rather roughly. She hit her, quite lightly at first, then harder a second time. Baby cried out with surprise and looked at her with hurt eyes.

Susy walked away, pleased. She went into the kitchen and deliberately spilt the food which he had prepared for Baby – some special mushy stuff that had no taste.

She went into the study, finding those typed sheets that were so precious to him, and she tore them and scattered the bits over the floor. The baby crawled in after her and began to chew the shreds.

Susy stepped over the baby, not caring now, bent on her path of destruction, all her unhappiness boiling over in a torrent of uncontrollable hatred.

She smashed vases, cups, a jug of water, trampled on his bed, wrecked a pile of clean shirts just back from the laundry, tore at the curtains, swept his photographs off the bureau. She was like a wild creature, her eyes gleaming, her pulse thudding, her breathing sharp and shallow.

The baby was at the foot of the stairs but Susy ran down, knocking her over in her flight. The baby started to cry but Susy did not care. She turned on her, wanting to hit her again. One of her long nails caught the baby's face, making her squeal in pain.

'Here! What's going on?'

Graham stood in the doorway, the key still in his hand.

Susy froze. His eyes went round the scene of destruction, finally taking in the baby who was still crying pitifully.

He turned to Susy. 'You wicked, wicked girl,' he said angrily, lifting his hand and striking her.

'Thank goodness I came back for my wallet. You might have killed the baby. I'll take her to Mrs Simons down the lane. She'll look after her for me while I'm away. I'm ashamed of you, Susy.'

He picked up the baby and began to soothe her.

Susy did not move. It was the first time he had struck her. She thought the world was falling to pieces around her. She stayed quite still, thinking perhaps he would hit her again and then she would die. But he did not touch her – he simply turned and walked out.

She ran away into the woods, and when he came back from London he called and searched in the garden and the woods beyond, but he could not find where she was hiding.

At last she could bear it no longer. She would accept his terms, share him, if only just to be with him sometimes and to love him.

She was thin and cold and hungry, and she went back to the cottage to ask him to take her back. He swept her into his arms, overjoyed that she had returned.

'Oh, Susy darling, I've missed you so much,' he said.

The weeks passed and the baby grew, and Susy still hated her, though now she hid this hatred inside, growing thinner as the baby grew fatter.

One day Graham came home from the market with someone and there were happy, laughing voices in the hall.

'Well, Val, this is it,' Graham was saying. 'What do you think of it? It's certainly not a palace, but at least Susy keeps it wholesome.'

'I think it's perfect,' said a woman's voice. 'Just the kind of cottage I've always dreamed about.'

'And you don't mind about Susy and Baby? Susy might break out again, you know.'

Curious, Susy came out of the kitchen and saw a tall young woman with loose, fair hair standing in the hall, close to Graham, holding his arm. Susy withdrew slightly, suddenly afraid, wondering what this man she loved was going to do now.

'Of course they hate each other,' the young woman said with a laugh. 'It's only natural. It's like having two women in one kitchen. They never get on.'

'Am I to take that as a hint that you don't want any other female in your kitchen?' Graham asked. They were smiling at each other.

'Nonsense,' she said. 'We'll keep Susy, of course. She obviously adores you. But the kitten will have to go. I'm sure my sister would have her.'

At that moment, the young woman caught sight of Susy behind the kitchen door and went to pick her up.

'Why, you beautiful thing,' said Val gently, stroking the long black fur. 'You are a lovely creature. Now you have two adoring females to spoil you,' she said to Graham, her eyes shining with happiness.

And Susy stretched deliciously in the young woman's arms, curling and uncurling her claws among the loose fair hair, purring a loud, rapturous welcome.

This was a woman after her own heart. Susy quite agreed. The kitten would have to go.

7 CURTAIN CALL

It was not that Titus was stagestruck or came of a theatrical family, but rather that he came upon the warm, steamy stage door entrance on a chilly October night when he was at his lowest ebb.

The Titus of that moment was far removed from the majestic creature that now greets patrons in the foyer of the plush Wellington Theatre as they arrive for the evening performance. He always sits a little to the side of the first step of the grand staircase leading to the Dress Circle, his brilliant lemon eyes scrutinising each new arrival.

But on that wet autumnal night, Titus slunk his emaciated body towards the stage door, drawn like a magnet towards the light and warmth. His black fur was matted, his white vest caked with Thames mud, one ear tattered and bloodied after a fight with some Soho cats over the debris from a restaurant dustbin.

Titus had been on the London streets for twenty-seven days. It had been a terrifying experience, and one for which his suburban upbringing had not prepared him. From kittenhood he had been housed by the Carson family, fed, milked and comfortably quartered in a specially designed cat-bed lined with foam cushions. Life had been uneventful apart from pouncing on the odd bird, or an occasional night-out caterwaul.

As Titus sunned himself in their back garden, he gathered vaguely that the Carsons were going on something called a holiday. He sensed change in the bustle of packing and kept out of the way. Then the Carsons discovered that the cat kennels had closed because of a flu epidemic.

This seemed to throw everyone in a panic, and Titus, who somehow felt responsible, kept very quiet and withdrawn. Then an old aunt appeared with an equally old wicker basket and said why couldn't they take Titus with them to the house they were renting in Cornwall?

Titus had sniffed the basket with apprehension. It smelled of long gone cats, ill cats, bored cats, tired cats. When they put him inside it, he fought and scratched and it took two adults to fasten the lid.

All the way to London in the car Titus spat and howled and they had to turn up the volume of the radio to drown his protests. Nerves began to get frayed and the children started to quarrel about silly things.

Titus scratched and chewed between howls. Suddenly the lid flew up and he scrambled out, perched for one petrified moment on the back of the driver's seat and then leaped out of the open car window. The cacophony was terrifying – buses, cars, coaches, hooters blaring from all directions . . . Titus fled along Westminster Bridge, careering between people's legs, dashing across the road, slithering down stone steps and racing along the Embankment, tail high, fur on end.

The Carsons could not find him. They spent an agonising two hours searching and calling his name. Eventually they gave up, reported their loss to the police, and continued on their way to Cornwall, both children crying noisily in the back of the car.

Titus crawled out from his hiding place under a fruit stall near Embankment underground station and surveyed the busy street scene. It was nothing like the town he came from. At first he felt a little heady and elated with his new freedom, and he strolled the streets, taking in everything like a tourist. He was somewhat bewildered by the sheer volume of traffic, but continued sight-seeing, curious and wondering.

However, three days later the excitement of city life had

worn off. He was cold and hungry, and had come across unexpected hostility from other vagrant cats. If he found a restaurant dustbin with some fish or chicken scraps in it, within seconds some huge alley-cat would turn up, hissing and spitting and claiming territorial rights.

The weather changed and it began to rain, and warm, dry places were difficult to find. The pavement was hard on his paws, and his pads grew callouses. The foam-cushioned bed began to fade from his memory.

Titus was not built for jungle warfare. His plump good looks quickly disappeared and he became scrawny and untrustful. No one spoke to him and he missed human companionship. No one stroked him with affection. His heart shrank with emptiness. Sometimes his only human contact was a boot kicking him out of a doorway.

He roamed the mud flats of the Thames shore, wondering if they might lead him to this place called Cornwall.

He had had nothing to eat all that twenty-seventh day except a rotting fish-head he had found in a gutter near Billingsgate Market, where the language addressed to him had not improved much since the sixteenth century.

He crouched against a wall where the overhanging stonework gave him some protection from the weather. His tail was curled under him, his ears flattened against his head. He watched the lights of the stage door entrance, and the orange-red glow from within. It looked warm and he could hear cheerful sounds.

People were coming out now, chatting and laughing, wrapping scarves round their heads and putting up brightly coloured umbrellas.

'Night-night. Sleep tight.'

'On my diet? See you tomorrow.'

Titus was wondering if he might be able to slip in unnoticed when the next group of people paused in the doorway before venturing out into the grey street. He slithered forward, his dark fur merging into the shadows of the night.

'Just look at that poor creature,' said one of the young women suddenly. She came out of the group, not conscious of the rain on her dark, curling hair. She did not touch

Titus, but went down on one knee, approaching him respectfully like a true cat lover.

She made small encouraging noises so that he would not be alarmed, and when he made no move to escape or bite, she put out a careful hand to rub his forehead.

'There, there, puss. My goodness, you are wet. And so thin. Look, Nigel, you can see his ribs. I don't think the poor thing has had a decent meal for weeks.'

'Oh, do come along, Lindy. Stop messing about with that revolting creature. You know we're meeting the others for supper, and we're going to be late as it is.' Nigel strolled over, a tall, elegant young man turning up the collar of his trench coat.

'It doesn't seem fair,' said Lindy, straightening up. 'Here we are, going out to supper when we're not really hungry, leaving this poor cat who is starving. It's cruel.'

'What do you propose to do? Take the cat out to supper with us? Do you think it would prefer Chinese or Italian?' he asked with a calculated degree of sarcasm in his voice. He was a very promising actor.

'That's a splendid idea,' said Lindy with some spirit. 'You go ahead and join the others. I'm taking him across to Joe's for a square meal. Don't wait for me.'

'You must be joking. Lindy, for heaven's sake, you're not going to pick it up? It's filthy and it's probably got fleas. It'll bite you and then you'll get tetanus. We've no one to replace you if you get ill,' Nigel warned gloomily.

'Nonsense, he's not going to bite me. He's got the look of a perfect gentleman. And you'd be filthy too, if you were living in the streets. He's a gorgeous cat really. Look at his eyes. They're beautiful . . . '

Titus did not struggle. The young woman's arms were holding him confidently, and her voice dripped words which were honey to his soul. Her eyes were a dark hazel, flecked with amber, warm, caring and unafraid.

Joe's Café was on the point of shutting, but when Joe saw Lindy approaching, he hastily reversed his closed sign.

'Hi,' he said, casually stacking his accountancy books out of sight under the counter. He was taking a correspondence course between customers. 'What can I get you?'

'One coffee and one warm milk straight away please, Joe. Then one cottage pie with plenty of gravy and I think I'll just have a cheese omelette,' said Lindy, choosing a table away from the door and the draughts. She settled the cat on her knee, calming his nerves with gentle strokes.

'Eating alone?' asked Joe, slightly confused by the order.

'No, just me and Titus,' said Lindy, making an equally puzzling reply.

How Titus enjoyed that first meal with Lindy! The warm milk was nectar, the cottage pie ambrosia. He could hardly eat for the deep, rhythmic purrs that threatened to choke him.

Afterwards Lindy took him back to the theatre, explaining that he could not live in her high-rise flat, but that he was welcome to doss down in her dressing room. She found him an old props box and lined it with a towel. She thoughtfully left open a small top window so that he could get in and out.

Titus fell asleep immediately, hardly able to believe his luck. He felt his dignity returning. He soon warmed to this strange, rambling building where people seemed to live during the day but went away at night when it became all his. Not only did he adopt the Wellington Theatre, but he appointed himself Lindy's guardian and mentor, too.

Taking charge of the theatre was a gargantuan task. He swept it clean of mice and no rats dared to come within a whisker of the place. He checked security, superintended the cleaning women, attended rehearsals, and was in the foyer every evening to welcome the patrons.

His appearance improved out of all recognition – he was not only clean and well-fed, but he had grown in magnificence with his new status. His black fur gleamed like darkest velvet, his white shirt front was whiter than pure snow and as soft as swansdown. He held his head proudly, his shoulders haunched haughtily, his tail curved over his toes with precision and delicacy. His lemon eyes watched everybody and everything: nothing escaped him, from a spider taking up residence behind a marble pedestal to a programme wedged between two seats.

Titus ate at Joe's Café and Lindy insisted that Joe gave her a weekly bill. Joe was reluctant about this, saying that Titus mainly ate leftovers, but Lindy was adamant. What about all the extra milk, she argued? Titus guessed that Joe did not charge Lindy enough because there was often a nice piece of fish or some steak for him. So he took on the café as a side line and the mice got a salutary eviction.

However, Titus had a curious attitude towards the cats who scavenged the dustbins. He did send them flying, but not, Joe observed, until after they had found something to eat.

'It's as if Titus remembers,' Joe told Lindy, one evening over a late coffee. 'He seems to have a certain sympathy for them.'

'Of course he remembers,' said Lindy, rubbing Titus expertly under his chin bone. 'Cats have memories, and are most intelligent creatures. Why, the Egyptians even worshipped a cat-goddess called Pasht.'

It was in Lindy's dressing room that Titus overheard Lindy and Nigel having a fairly heated discussion about the play. It was a classic thriller and assured of a pretty long run with the tourists and coach parties. But Lindy was unhappy about one scene.

'The letter incident really is my best scene,' Lindy was saying as she sat at the mirror taking off her make-up. 'And I would appreciate it if you would not fidget so much, Nigel. Somehow it destroys the tension I'm trying to build up.'

Titus was only half listening. He was curled up in his prop box which by now was lined with Lindy's shawl.

'I'm not fidgeting,' said Nigel, lighting up a cigarette. 'I'm merely being natural and at ease.'

'I don't regard that messing about with the decanter this evening as being natural and at ease. How can I be tense and emotional, reading the letter, when you are wandering about doing different things? It wouldn't be so bad if you always did the same things, then at least I could time my pauses.'

'I'm improvising, darling,' said Nigel, casually. 'You should be able to cope.'

Lindy turned, the amber in her eyes starting to spark. She crunched the tissue in her hand and tossed it into the wastepaper bin.

'I don't rush about madly during your confession scene,' she retorted. 'I keep still, I blend, I merge. I leave it to you. It's your scene.'

'But that's your style,' said Nigel, getting up to leave. 'You blend, merge . . . I just naturally dominate.'

'Oh!' The crash as she slammed down the jar of cleansing cream made Titus almost jump out of his box. 'How can you be so selfish?' Lindy stormed at Nigel. 'You're spoiling my best part. People will stop believing in me, and then when the c-contracts are renewed, they'll get s-somebody else . . . and I'll be out on the streets.'

Titus did not understand about contracts, but he knew all about being out on the streets. He had had twenty-seven days of it and he would not wish one half-minute of the experience on his beloved Lindy.

The following evening, once the audience was seated and he had checked the stalls, the dress circle and the upper circle, Titus sat in the wings, keeping well out of everyone's way.

It was true. During the letter scene, Nigel very craftily took the tension out of Lindy's reading. He stretched, he got up to close the curtains, he smoothed his hair in a mirror . . .

Lindy's hand was trembling as she held the crucial letter but Titus could tell that the audience had been diverted and the atmosphere in the theatre had lost its electricity.

In the interval he went back to Lindy's dressing room but he did not go in. From inside he could hear the sound of weeping. He quickly nipped over to Joe's Café to try and seek help there. Joe looked up from the text book he was studying, surprised, since Titus never usually left the theatre during a performance.

'Hello, you're early,' he said. 'What's the matter?'

Titus could not tell him, but he tried. He rubbed against Joe's ankles, miaowing desperately. Realising he wasn't having any luck with Joe, he returned swiftly to the theatre.

The confession scene was near the end of the play. It was

well-written and Nigel made the most of it. He began the speech with his usual confident skill.

At about line four, Titus casually strolled on stage. He sniffed carefully around and then decided that the upholstered arm of the settee was the best vantage point. He leapt up gracefully and got into position. Then he turned and stared at Nigel.

He stared. He kept still. He remembered what Lindy had said about blending, but it was a little difficult for a magnificent black and white shorthaired cat to blend successfully.

He sat there throughout the whole speech, staring, dignified, enigmatic, ears pricked at such an angle that he looked as though he were listening politely to a vaguely amiable idiot.

Nigel fought back. His voice grew louder, his projection more deliberate. The sweat glistened on his forehead.

Then Titus yawned, a small pink-mouthed yawn of delicate boredom. The audience collapsed in laughter.

It did not ruin the play but it did ruin Nigel's scene. He stormed off after the curtain calls in a furious temper.

'I'll kill that cat,' he raged. 'Get it out of the theatre!'

But the management refused. Everyone liked Titus. The producer thought the change of emphasis actually improved the finale. He was wondering if Titus could be persuaded to do it again.

Meanwhile Titus took refuge under a table at Joe's, exhausted. Acting was definitely tiring work. And those blinding bright lights. . . the experience had been quite unnerving.

Of course it was in all the newspapers the next day, and soon the box office began to break records as people flocked to see Titus. He did not always go on. It seemed to depend on how the letter scene went, observed Joe, who came over regularly to watch the phenomenon.

Eventually Nigel's nerve broke. He could stand it no longer and he left the cast. Lindy got her contract renewed, Joe passed his exams and a few months later they got married.

Titus was guest-of-honour at the wedding reception. He

decided wedding cake was overrated but champagne was delicious. Lindy looked as pretty as a picture with white roses entwined in her dark curls, and he hardly recognised Joe in a suit.

'And where are you going for your honeymoon?' someone asked.

'Cornwall,' said Lindy. 'We've been lent a very romantic fisherman's cottage. We thought we might take Titus with us.'

Titus did a standing leap which took him out of the window on to the balcony of the restaurant. He fled down the Strand, through the back streets of Covent Garden, down an alleyway that led to another alleyway that led to the back of the theatre, up through his window into Lindy's dressing room and into his prop box.

He loved Lindy. He was prepared to follow her to the ends of the earth. But there was one place where he would not go.

8 TUFTY'S HORSE

Seven-year-old Howard eyed his lunch with distaste. Casseroled chicken, carrots, onions, creamed swede, potatoes, there was nothing there he really liked except the spuds. He looked calculatingly at his mother, not appreciating her young dark looks and fresh yellow dress, but trying to size up from her expression just how much she would allow him to leave on his plate.

Howard knew there was the most delicious apple sponge to follow because he had seen her making it that morning. He also knew that he would not get any if he left his first course.

He sighed. Life was hard. He dug his toe into the soft fur of his kitten, Candy, who was asleep under the table, and wondered if he could slip her any of the chicken without being noticed. Candy liked chicken.

His sister, Jane, four and solemn, with stubby slow-growing pigtails, sat opposite him at the table, plying her knife and fork with the concentration of a gourmet.

'For goodness' sake,' said Lisa, exasperated by her son's unwillingness to eat. 'Do get on with your lunch. It's getting cold and you know we're going to see Grandma this afternoon.'

'I don't like it,' Howard mumbled, pushing morsels relentlessly round his plate with his fork.

Candy awoke from the prodding toe, stretched herself and padded daintily over to Jane's kitten, Tufty. The children had two kittens, both black. But Candy was small, appealing and pretty, while Tufty was already growing into a big clown, always falling over his own paws, chasing his tail idiotically, boxing his own shadow on the wall, his long black fur sticking out wildly at all angles.

'You don't know what's good for you,' said Jim, his father.

Jane let the argument flow over her. She was watching the kittens playing on the carpet, rolling over and biting into each other's soft necks. When the kittens had arrived, Mummy had given the girl kitten to Howard and the boy kitten to Jane, which was all very sad for secretly it was Candy she loved, the sweet little female.

How Jane loved and longed for her, with her dainty doll-like ways, tiny blue-eyed face and minute whiskers. And yet she was supposed to love and look after Tufty, a great fool who just rushed about the house like a mad thing, with stuck up fur and big ears and nothing pretty about him at all.

Jane felt the tears of her unspoken love welling up and burning her eyelids. She blinked hard. She had tried to persuade Howard to swop kittens, but he had refused. He too preferred the appeal of the smaller one.

'Swop? Of course I don't want to swop,' he had said firmly, stroking the neat little Candy under her chin till her tiny, melodious purr threatened to engulf her throat. 'For that untidy old Tufty? He looks more like a hedgehog than a cat. Me, swop? Not likely.'

Jim put down his knife and fork and looked first at his watch and then at his stubborn son. 'You have exactly five minutes, my boy. Now eat your lunch or go hungry.'

Howard stared at his chilling plate. 'Chicken – white and stringy and horrid,' he mumbled.

Jim was about to burst into a lecture when he caught Lisa's eye. She hated scenes, especially at meal times. He decided to ignore the challenge.

'Chicken? But that's not chicken,' said Jim casually. 'Don't you know the difference? That's elephant meat.'

'Elephant meat?' Howard's eyes went round and incredulous.

'Yes, elephant meat. Caught it in the garden this morning.'

'You didn't. . . '

'Well, no, I didn't personally catch it,' said Jim with a shrug. 'I was busy with the bonfire, but along came this elephant. Quite a small one, actually, and. . . er. . . '

'Tufty caught it,' said Lisa quietly.

Jane looked up in surprise. 'Tufty?'

Lisa nodded. 'Mmm. Tufty. You know Tufty's a great hunter. Well, this morning he went out and caught an elephant.'

Jane stopped eating to think about this for a moment. 'But an 'nelephant's *'normous,'* she said suspiciously.

'Tufty shook out his fur until he was twice his normal size, growled fiercely at the elephant and chased him all over the garden. He never gave up. He's such a great hunter,' said Lisa.

Jane thrust out her lower lip in disbelief. 'Tufty couldn't run after 'nelephant. 'Nelephant got 'normous legs,' she said loudly.

'That's true,' agreed Lisa. 'We all know that elephants are enormous. That's why Tufty went on his horse.'

'On his horse?!' Howard's voice spiralled up to a squeak. 'Tufty on a horse?'

Howard's face was agog, a forkful of hated carrot half-way to his open mouth. Jane sat straight and still, an inner battle going on inside her against the tiny seed of admiration sown for Tufty.

'I don't believe Tufty's got a horse,' she said at last.

'Oh yes, he has,' said Lisa airily. She glanced across to her husband. He was silently choking. 'He keeps it in the cellar.'

Jim coughed and spluttered, and then Howard saw the way his parents were smiling at each other, and suddenly, to his intense delight, he knew. His face went pink with pleasure.

'You're tricking me,' Jane protested to the other three.

'No, we're not!' Howard shouted, his eyes bright with excitement. 'He keeps it in the cellar. Didn't you know that? I knew it all the time, silly.'

Jim tried hard to control his laughter. He leaned over to his small solemn daughter. 'You know every time we see Tufty flying past the window?' Jane nodded slowly, uncertainly. . . 'Well, really he's sitting on his horse. Because of the window-sill, and the horse being low down, it's only Tufty we see. But actually he's sitting on his horse.'

'And he's got a cowboy hat,' added Howard, almost convulsed by his own wit. 'With two holes in it for his ears to poke through.'

Jane shot a venomous look at Howard. But she was not sure about her father. . .

'Tufty keeps his horse in the cellar, Jane,' Lisa explained quickly, 'because he's very shy about having a horse. After all, it's not every cat that's got a horse, is it? Candy doesn't have one. Girl kittens don't have horses.'

'I see. . . ' said Jane, who didn't. 'And girl cats aren't great hunters, are they, mummy?'

'That's right, so they don't need a horse. But Tufty's a great hunter and he needs a horse.'

The great hunter espied a mote of dust floating in a ray of sunlight and hurled himself at it, skidding on the polished floor, landing in a big clumsy heap hard up against the foot of the bookcase. He blinked his large surprised yellow eyes and shook out the ruff round his neck. He caught sight of the crumpled rug and stalked it slowly, stealthily, his long fluffy tail thumping the floor in mock rage. . .

Jane finished her dinner thoughtfully. 'Can I see this horse in the cellar?' she asked.

Jim raised his eyebrows fractionally. Get yourself out of this one it signalled to his wife.

'Now that might be a little difficult,' said Lisa. 'You see, we can only see this horse in the dark. It's extremely shy, and as soon as we put the light on in the cellar, it disappears, as quick as a flash, into the coal hole.'

'Into the coal hole?' repeated Jane, with all the scorn that a four-year-old could muster. 'But a horse is much too big to go into the coal hole.'

'Don't you know anything, stupid,' crowed Howard triumphantly. 'It's not an ordinary horse. It's a cat's horse, of course!'

Everybody started to talk at once. Jane wanted to know the truth but how could she? It was all too confusing. Lisa began to clear the plates, not commenting on Howard's passable effort in that direction. She brought out the well-risen apple sponge and a jug of custard, and smiled at the puzzlement on her small daughter's face. She wanted to believe in the horse; she wanted to believe that Tufty was a great and intrepid hunter. But she was a sensible child and her brain cells were working overtime telling her all this couldn't possibly be true. . .

After the meal, Jane got down and went round to her mother. She put her arms round her.

'Will you show me Tufty's horse?'

Lisa opened the cellar door as quietly as she could, feeling Jane's small fingers gripping her hand tightly. It was not fair, she thought with compassion, to tease the little girl to this extent. But it was too late to turn back now. It had to be acted out. She did not want the episode to end in tears.

'I can't see anything,' Jane whispered, peering down the steps into the darkness. 'Where is he?'

'He's usually in front of the boiler,' Lisa whispered back. She put her hand on the switch and suddenly the cellar was flooded with light. 'Oh dear, he's gone,' said Lisa casually. 'Too late. Never mind, Jane.' Lisa drew back. 'Let's get ready to go out. We're going to Grandma's, remember? That'll be nice.'

Jane thought about Tufty's horse all the way to Grandma's, and she even told her Grandma about it.

'My kitten, Tufty, has got a horse,' Jane informed her.

'Oh, how lovely for him,' said Grandma, who couldn't hear very well.

It was dark and very quiet in the house when Jane woke up and wanted to go to the bathroom. She padded sleepily out of her room on to the landing in her striped pyjamas and thought how lonely the house was in the middle of the night. It must be very, very late.

But there was a gleam of light from under Mummy's bedroom door which meant that Daddy was probably reading in bed as he often did. It was comforting to think that they were both there, and if she wanted anything she only had to call.

The old house rustled and creaked, and on her way back to her room Jane suddenly thought of Tufty's horse. Of course! This was the very time to catch it there in the cellar. It would be asleep and wouldn't have time to wake up and dash into the coal hole. She would be sure to see it this time!

She crept down the stairs, her heart beating furiously. The cellar door creaked as she opened it. A furry softness touched her bare ankle. Jane jumped back with a frightened gasp, but then in the moonlight from the window she saw that it was only Tufty. She picked him up, grateful for some company.

She felt her way carefully down the wooden steps, and put her hand slowly over the cold metal lightswitch at the bottom. She was trembling, her mouth dry with fear. The kitten, suddenly feeling unsafe, started to struggle, and as she tried to hold him still with one hand, his claw flashed out and drew a long scratch down her hand.

Quickly she switched on the light.

There was nothing. Nothing at all. Only the boiler, a pile of chopped wood for starting the boiler, Mummy's empty jam jars, and an old kitchen table that they no longer used.

Relief swept through Jane. She hadn't really wanted to find a snorting, stamping, pawing four-legged horse, however small, in their cellar. She hugged Tufty to her, stroking his funny big ears.

'But I'm sure you could catch an elephant if you wanted to,' she whispered into his soft neck. She felt all the tickly softness of his ruff on the end of her nose. He began to purr. It was an enormous, joyous sound and Jane's heart began to swell with love for him.

At breakfast the next morning, Jane waited until there was a break in the family chatter to announce her news.

'I've seen Tufty's horse,' she said at last, rather loudly.

There was an astonished silence while Jane held out her hand. It was bound with a ragged piece of pink sticking plaster.

She waggled her hand proudly.

'And he bit me,' she said.

9 A CATASTROPHIC PERSON

It always took Grace a considerable time to walk along Oakleigh Road because she had so many friends to say hello to on the way. She would never dream of slighting an old friend, or a new one, even if it made the difference between catching the 8.15 am to Victoria Station and missing it.

First there was Mabel. Mabel was a smoky grey Persian with tabby markings, the prettiest little face and BO. She waited permanently on the pavement for the admiration and caresses which she considered her due.

A few houses further down was Susie, who was black, sleek and had three legs after a road accident. She was pathetically grateful for attention and would hop frantically through the flowerbeds at the sound of Grace calling her name. Susie made little of her disability but she never attempted to cross a road again. She stayed on her own side, her world reduced to a few acres of garden surrounded by a border of tarmac.

Titch was also black and sleek, but with four legs and a velvet sheen on her coat that spoke volumes about her well-fed, pampered life. However, Titch came of a theatrical family and her favourite role was that of a homeless, starving waif thrown out on to the pavement. Her acting was pretty good, and she managed to fool a lot of people.

'Poor Titch,' Grace would murmur, sympathetically

stroking a forlorn ear. 'Have they all gone out and left you again? And did they forget to give you your breakfast? You'll have to catch yourself a mouse.'

Thomas was a thug-faced ginger tom who spent most of the day guarding cars. He sat on a car roof top, barely acknowledging Grace's friendly greeting although his timid heart yearned to respond. He was too shy even to run away. Whereas Sheba, the pale Siamese next door, spoke to no one, not even other cats, and hid in hedges perfecting her vocal imitation of a baby.

Grace never ignored any cat and this left her breathless by the time she reached the station and stumbled into a carriage. Hugh held the door open with an expression of amused tolerance on his handsome face. He helped her aboard.

'Nearly missed it again,' he said. 'All those damned cats, I suppose.'

'Susie can't hurry,' said Grace. 'And I'd hate to miss her out. It's a miracle she's still alive.'

'Ridiculous to go to all that trouble for a cat. They should have had her put down,' said Hugh complacently.

'How would you like it if you had a road accident and someone decided not to bother to patch you up?' asked Grace, with a trace of anger in her low voice.

'Don't be silly,' said Hugh, only half listening. 'People aren't cats.'

But cats are like people, Grace thought. 'And I'm cultivating Thomas,' she said aloud. 'That takes time.'

She was between cats at the moment, and that meant she had a special need for the unconditional affection so generously offered by cat friends. Even the distant Thomas and the vanishing Sheba were reassuringly themselves and a challenge for Grace's incurable ailurophilia.

Grace sighed as she settled back into a seat and Hugh opened the *Financial Times*. She had been going out with Hugh for nearly a year. He was good company, intelligent, successful at his job as an accountant, and, for some reason totally unknown to Grace, he had singled her out from all the other local girls.

Grace never really could understand why. There was a

shortage of men in their area and Grace had felt it more acutely because of her height – her five feet eight inches immediately put off half the male population. Hugh was an easy six feet and she had been captivated from the moment she fell over his feet getting on the train one morning. His dark eyes seemed to radiate warmth and sensuality; his hand steadying her arm had sent shivers down her spine; his dark brown voice rendered her speechless.

'Are you feeling all right?' he had enquired as he dusted off his hand-stitched brown shoes.

'Oh yes. . . ' Grace had breathed. She had never felt better.

However, Grace soon discovered that she had a price to pay for Hugh's favours. She had to conform to the kind of behaviour Hugh expected from a young woman. She had to tone down her disco dancing from its normal wild abandon, put away her outlandish gear and wear restrained dresses and skirts. She had to go lightly with the kohl round her eyes – Hugh thought that too much make-up was vulgar.

Grace played a good game of tennis and Hugh liked having her for a partner. She had the height and reach, but Hugh soon discovered that she lacked concentration, particularly if a certain tabby kitten was around the tennis club.

'Hello, Little Mo,' said Grace, stooping to stroke the little stray who had attached herself to the club for the season. Little Mo seemed to live on bar food, crisps and cold sausages, so Grace often brought her the odd tit-bit in a margarine tub.

'It's your service,' Hugh hollered.

'Sorry,' said Grace, throwing the ball into the air. 'Little Mo feels hurt if I don't speak to her. She gets quite lonely at times.'

The kitten danced across the court, bouncing after the ball, her tail a streaming banner. Hugh missed his return shot.

'You're the most impossible person I have ever come across,' said Hugh, removing the kitten. 'How can you tell if a cat's feelings are hurt? Tell me that.'

'She looks hurt,' said Grace defiantly.

'With all those stripes on her face, I fail to see how you can detect any expression. Really Grace, it's time you grew up.'

'Please stay off the court,' Grace whispered to Little Mo, wrapping the kitten in her cardigan and putting her on a sunny chair. Her blue eyes blinked lovingly and she immediately went to sleep.

They played well and won the match. Hugh was pleased.

'That's my girl,' he said, throwing an arm round Grace's shoulders and bending to brush the lobe of her ear with his lips. Grace almost stopped breathing. This had to be what she had been waiting for all her life. It was chemistry, magnetism, sex-appeal, any word would do. . . but it was still a magical something that made Grace try to change in order to please Hugh.

However, there was nothing much she could do about the cats. She had loved cats all her walking days, and she could not ignore them even to keep Hugh.

'For goodness sake, come along Grace,' said Hugh, as they hurried along Oakleigh Road. 'We'll miss the beginning of the film.'

Grace caught him up, a little breathless. 'I will not pass Susie without saying hello,' she said. 'She has a very uneventful life with only three legs.'

'And you think your two-seconds worth makes a difference to her?' Hugh commented wryly.

'It's a human contact. Without this vital contact, her life would become dry and empty.'

'Nonsense,' said Hugh. 'I've never yet met a cat that wasn't snooty and offhand.'

Grace almost said that was because he was snooty and offhand, but she bit back the words. Sometimes she wished he was not quite so perfect for her in every other way.

It was with these sobering thoughts that Grace walked to the station the next morning. She was not sure that she wanted to change the way Hugh proposed. She could change herself on the surface, but beneath her lady-like exterior she would still be the girl she had always been.

Thomas, the thug-faced ginger tom, was sitting on the

roof of a soft-topped sports car. She stopped and reached up to scratch his furry ear. He arched his back, embarrassed.

'Don't be shy, darling,' she said gently. 'I want to make friends.'

'And I'd like to be your friend, too.'

'How extraordinary,' said Grace, recovering her composure. 'I didn't know Thomas could speak.'

A tousled head of unruly hair appeared from beneath the car, then a face streaked with grease grinned up at her. The young man looked at Grace with admiration in his bright blue eyes.

'We don't tell everyone,' he said. 'Not even the neighbours.'

'I was actually talking to your cat,' Grace explained formally, her hand resting lightly on Thomas's furry neck. He moved imperceptibly, half an inch forward.

'My mother's cat. I'm Pete Hardy. I'm home on leave from the army. I don't think we've met but we should have. Thomas is slipping – I rely on him for introductions.'

'He's very shy,' said Grace. 'It's taken me months to get this far.'

Pete scrambled out from under the car and brushed the bits off his jeans. 'I promise I won't be so slow,' he grinned.

'I shall have to go,' said Grace. 'If I talk to people as well, I shall miss my train.' She noticed they were the same height.

'Hop in. I'll give you a lift to the station.' He scooped Thomas off the roof and deposited him on a flowerbed. 'Do some gardening for a change,' he suggested to the cat.

Grace was not late for her train that morning. Hugh noted her even breathing. There was not a strand of red-streaked hair out of place. She looked almost serious.

'No cats this morning?' he enquired.

'Only one,' she said. 'The shy one.'

He squeezed her hand encouragingly. 'That's my girl,' he said. 'You're showing some sense at last.'

The last dance of the season was a special evening in the tennis club calendar. Hugh and Grace danced together all evening. She floated in his arms, very aware of his closeness, the spicy fragrance of his aftershave, the smoothness of his cheek so close to her own. It was a wonderful evening and Grace began to think of a lifetime of such bliss. Perhaps Hugh was right when he said she was immature . . . perhaps it would be easy to change if she could always be so happy . . .

Then the music quickened to disco and Grace promptly broke a heel dancing to the latest chart success. She hobbled off the floor, the offending spike in her hand.

'You're hopeless,' said Hugh, putting the heel in his pocket. They walked outside the clubhouse, their arms entwined. The music was still playing, the air full of pale blossoms swaying in the silvery moonlight. It was a perfect evening. The last of summer. Hugh took Grace into his arms and her mouth was warm and sweet as he kissed her.

As Grace soared in the heady sensation of his embrace, far away she heard a small, faint sound. At first it hardly registered, but then she heard it again and moved hesitantly away from his seeking mouth.

'Grace . . . what is it?' he murmured against her face. 'Don't go . . . please.'

'I thought I heard something. It came from over there . . . '

'It was nothing. An owl, a mouse . . . '

'No, it wasn't. I think something is hurt . . . I must find out.' She twisted out of his arms and began to search the darkened car park, limping with her shoeless foot.

'Grace . . . come back. You can't do anything.'

'But I can hear something crying . . . '

Grace almost stumbled over a small dark shape stretched out on the driveway. It was Little Mo, the stray kitten. She had been hit by a car and her back legs were unnaturally still. There was blood in her nostrils, and she was crying piteously and uncomprehendingly.

Grace crouched over the injured animal, her heart pounding. 'Poor baby,' she moaned. 'Poor Little Mo.'

The little creature looked smaller than ever, its face pointed and bony with pain. She tried to drag her back legs but there was no support in them.

'We must do something,' Grace shivered. 'It's the little tabby kitten,' she called to Hugh. 'She's badly hurt. Some stupid driver . . . '

'It's only a stray. She'll be dead by the morning,' said Hugh, strolling over and looking down at the mutilated animal. 'Come back to the clubhouse. I'll buy you a drink. You look pale.'

Grace was aghast. 'We can't just leave her. She's in terrible pain, poor little thing. She's suffering and she doesn't understand what's happened to her. All she knows is something's not right and she's frightened.'

'It's only a cat,' said Hugh, exasperated. 'You make her sound like a human being.'

'I'm going to find someone who will help if you won't,' said Grace fiercely. 'Someone with feeling. Someone with a heart and not just a handsome face.'

'You're impossible,' said Hugh, his profile immovable in the moonlight. 'All this fuss over a stray cat. I don't understand you.'

Grace limped up the steps into the clubhouse. She knew who she was looking for. Pete was not dancing, but talking in a crowd by the bar. He looked tough and dependable, the aggressive line of his jaw softened by the humour in his eyes. He was still in jeans, a cleaner pair perhaps, with an old, faded combat shirt. He saw Grace and left the group immediately.

'What's the matter?' he asked.

'It's Little Mo. She's been run over and she's very badly hurt. I don't know . . . perhaps we could take her to a vet, or something.' Grace swallowed hard. 'She's in such pain . . . '

'Show me,' said Pete.

The world shrank. Grace could only think of the pain, the small heartrending cries, the stillness . . . Grace hid her face. She could not look. It was all over in moments. The crying ceased.

The music was playing again and the soft, balmy air was filled with the scent of blossom. It was all unreal, the music, the dancing, the passionate kisses she had shared with

Hugh. Reality was the pain and bewilderment of a little cat.

Grace knew she could not change. She would always be this kind of person, a little impossible to live with but not if the man really loved her. And if there were not enough men to go round, then she would make her own home and live by herself . . . well, not quite by herself. There might be a cat or two . . .

'Would you like to walk home?' said Pete. 'I can fetch my car in the morning. You can borrow my tennis shoes.'

'Yes, I would like that,' said Grace, hardly audible.

They did not talk. They walked slowly through the coolness of the night, the street lamps throwing their orange glow on to the pavements. A small grey shadow detached itself from the darkness and wound itself round Grace's ankles.

'Oh, Mabel,' said Grace, with instant recognition. 'You do need a bath. Hasn't your best friend told you?'

Susie leaped off a low wall and landed a little unsteadily on her three paws. She was delighted and surprised to see Grace so late and purred loudly.

'Hello, Susie,' said Grace in a trembling voice. 'You survived all right, didn't you? Not like Little Mo.'

'Little Mo was too badly hurt. No one could have done anything,' Pete began.

'Yes, I know,' said Grace, walking on.

Titch was sitting on the top step outside her house. She had only been out five minutes but she managed to make it look as though she had been there hours. Grace had to smile.

'Cheer up, beautiful,' she said. 'They'll let you in again soon.'

They stopped outside Grace's house. She turned to Pete, wanting to say something.

'I'm between cats at the moment,' she said. 'I was going to bring Little Mo home for the winter.'

'I know. I know . . . ' he said.

He did not take her hand or touch her. There was no magic or chemistry. But there was something else. . . a tiny feeling of awareness that had nothing to do with sex and everything to do with love.

Thomas was sitting on top of a van. He had been trying to make up his mind all day. But here she was and she had not seen him. If he did not hurry, she would be gone and then it would be too late.

He leaped off the van and ran across the road, his heart pounding. Even now he dared not come too close, but hesitated some yards away with a little sidestep.

But Grace had seen him. She went down on one knee and held out her hand. He sniffed it cautiously. Grace did not move or speak, knowing that they had come to the moment of trust. And trust was the beginning of love.

10 THE PRINCESS AND THE PAUPER

As soon as she came into the compound, he realised that she was not among the ordinary run of visitors. There were no children tugging this way and that at her hand. She was not making various cooing noises. She did not flutter ecstatically by the first large cage of adorably fluffy kittens . . .

Purposefully the young woman approached the row of cages housing adult cats, her air of calm efficiency only slightly impaired by the tension in her slim neck. She was pretty in a flower-like way, but with strength in her delicate features, a contradiction that gave her face character. She looked along the line of cages.

'Oh heavens,' she murmured, somewhat distraught.

There were dozens of cats. Fat ones, thin ones, old ones, young ones. Pairs of green, blue and yellow eyes swivelled away from her. They ignored visitors. She was merely part of the daily procession.

But he knew she was someone different. He sensed the hidden distress as the young woman swiftly progressed towards him. She stopped and looked into his cage, a sudden gleam of hope coming into her clear hazel eyes.

'Now, you might do,' she said. She turned to the kennel maid who had been following her. 'Can you tell me anything about this one?'

The kennel maid, who was a sturdy youth of nineteen, had all the facts. 'For a start,' he said, 'we get very few

Seal-points. Most Siamese owners take good care of their animals. But the circumstances here are a little unusual. The owner was an elderly lady, a Mrs Ferguson from somewhere in Australia. She left the Siamese in six months' quarantine when she came back to England, presumably to spend her last days in this country.'

'An Australian Siamese. How interesting!'

'Well, apparently they must really have been her last days, for no Mrs Ferguson ever turned up to collect her cat.'

'Have you tried to trace her?'

'Of course, people have tried, but with no success. There's a bill of several hundred pounds outstanding at the boarding establishment.'

'What's the cat's name? Have you got its papers?'

The youth coloured slightly. 'Er . . . unfortunately, no. The relevant papers became detached from the cat during its transfer to the refuge.'

Fiona was inspecting the animal closely. It had a cream-coloured body, shading to a pale, warm fawn on the back, with mask, ears, legs, feet and tail of dark brown. There was a good width between its eyes, its ears were well pricked. It gazed at her fathomlessly with its brilliant blue eyes, oriental in shape but with no squint.

'The mask is a little dark,' she murmured.

'We usually only keep 'em seven days, but this is such a beautiful cat.' It was blatant sales talk.

'OK. I think she'll do.'

'He's a neutered male.'

'Oh heavens!' The young woman was torn, then something in the Siamese's dignified expression made up her mind. He was too proud to remind her of the six months already spent in lonely quarantine, or of the fate that awaited him soon if he remained homeless. But it was there in his eyes. He looked intelligent and she desperately needed intelligent help.

'Do I have to sign something?'

'Come to the office,' said the kennel person, thrusting his hands into the pockets of his overall. 'You've got a good 'un there.'

The Siamese was put into a cardboard cat box and Fiona took him out to her car. Once inside with the windows closed, she opened the lid. He stepped out cautiously.

'I don't like these boxes,' said Fiona. 'Do you think you could manage to keep still while I drive us home?'

He listened. He'd been in a car before, couldn't she tell? He sat down on the front seat and began to groom himself meticulously. He did not turn a hair when she switched on the engine and drove slowly out of the compound.

'I have to tell you that your name is Princess Mila,' said Fiona with some trepidation. 'I know it sounds a stupid name, but it's only a collection of syllables after all. If it's all right with you, I think I'll call you Prinny. Perhaps you'll get used to it. But I wish we knew your real name. If only you could tell me.'

Prinny sat very still awaiting events. He was so damned glad to be out of that cage that he did not really care where this nice young woman took him or what she called him.

'We live in a house near Kensington Gardens,' she went on. 'I think you'll like it. At least, it's not my house. I work there as a sort of housekeeper-come-secretary. It's my responsibility to see that everything runs smoothly. The main advantage of the job is that I have my own small flat at the top of the house, and in these days that's like gold dust. I couldn't afford to live anywhere in London at today's prices.'

Prinny gave a low miaow to show his understanding. He was enjoying the ride and his driver's gentle voice. He noticed that the delicate spring leaves were bursting out on the trees again and little clouds were chasing each other across the sky. He liked seeing children skipping along the pavements, the other cars flashing by with powerful roars, the lumbering red buses towering overhead while he sat safe and contained in this funny little square car. He trusted Fiona implicitly. There were some people that could be trusted straight away. Yet she had not touched him once yet. It was all in her voice.

'Poor puss,' she was saying. 'What a long time to be shut away. It must have been horrid. I suppose you have almost forgotten Mrs Ferguson by now.'

He felt compelled to tell her that he had not forgotten Mrs Ferguson, nor ever would. But Fiona did not know him well enough to understand or recognise his different vowel sounds.

Prinny looked curiously at his new home – an elegant Georgian town house in a square of other elegant Georgian town houses, very different from the rambling Australian ranch on which he had once lived. He padded over the priceless Persian carpet in the polished hallway, and sniffed at the burst of bright yellow daffodils arranged in a crystal vase on the Sheraton table. He felt sure the young woman had put them there.

Is this it, he yeowelled?

'This is it,' said Fiona. 'And, believe it or not, you have a sitting room of your very own. Now how many pussycats can boast of that? See what you think of it.'

Fiona opened a door to one of the ground floor rooms. It was furnished like a normal sitting room, but there were a few feline refinements. There was a cushion-lined cat bed on four short gilt legs. A grooming table. A china bowl of water standing on a king-sized mat. A cat litter-tray was discreetly hidden behind a screen. The room was centrally heated and the double-glazed glass doors lead out on to a small but richly-green lawn. On the wall hung a cabinet containing a collection of satin rosettes and several silver cups.

Wow, said Prinny, impressed.

He also immediately knew a lot about the other cat that had once lived there. She scratched and sharpened her claws on the legs of the grooming table. She adored minced chicken and warm milk. She was lazy and sat about a lot, especially on the chair with the satin cushions. The doors to the room had not been opened for a long time.

'I want you to stay indoors for a few days,' said Fiona. 'I'm sorry about it, but I'd hate you to run away or get lost.'

Prinny shrugged his compliance. He would have agreed to anything at that moment. Anyway, there was plenty to look at around the house.

'You can roam all over until she comes back. Would you

like to see the kitchen and my office? Then I'll get you some milk. Come along, Prinny.'

Prinny followed her neat ankles along a mirror-lined corridor to the back kitchen. He did a complicated little side step as he crossed over the threshold – a sort of celebration dance. It was a very modern room, not at all like the kitchen at the ranch, but nevertheless it had a more lived-in atmosphere than the rest of the house. In a room leading off the kitchen there was a desk and a typewriter. The room smelt of flowers and the young woman.

'This is my office. You can come and see me anytime.'

He leaped up on to the desk and walked all over her papers, which rustled delightfully. He smelled the mysterious innards of her typewriter. His ears pricked as he heard a thrush somewhere in the garden singing loud and clear, a tantalising sound. He turned and gazed longingly at Fiona. Can I, he asked, please . . .

She shook her head. 'Sorry, Prinny. No birds allowed. It's a rule. Come and have some milk while I make myself a cup of tea.'

Prinny sat beside the saucer she had given him. He had no taste for English milk; now Australian milk, that was different. He waited patiently then he tapped her arm. She was stirring her cup of tea.

'Why, I do believe you would rather have some tea,' she laughed. She got a clean saucer and poured him some from the teapot. He began to paw the ground as she put it down for him, but he still did not touch it.

'Sugar?' she inquired.

That night he did not sleep in the cushioned bed. He chewed a corner thoughtfully, then decided to curl up under the radiator. He had also ignored the chicken dinner, preferring to share Fiona's scrambled eggs and bacon in the kitchen.

The next morning he was exploring the rooms on the first floor when he heard a car draw up outside the house. He peered down from the windowsill and saw a large purple-ribboned hat being helped out of the car and then coming up the front steps. The ribbons wobbled as the hat laboured up the steps.

Fiona rushed into the room, her brown hair flying, picked Prinny up and hurried downstairs to his sitting-room. He lay stiffly in her arms, like a bundle of brown sticks. Did he have to go back to the refuge? It could only be bad news . . .

'Now you've got to be very, very good,' she whispered urgently. 'Mrs Armitage is back and you know what she's like.' Then Fiona did a very peculiar thing. She patted his face with some fine white stuff that made him sneeze. 'Don't fuss,' she pleaded, shielding his eyes with her other hand. 'It's only talcum powder. Your muzzle is a little too dark.'

She put him on to the satin cushions.

'Sit,' she hissed. He was so surprised, he did.

Under the large purple-ribboned hat was a large purple-ribboned woman, and suddenly Prinny found himself clasped and squeezed against ample folds of purple bosom. He was too astonished to resist.

'Princess, my darling Princess. Mummy's back! Has my darling Princess missed her Mummy while she's been away in America?'

Prinny yeowelled politely. What a strange woman!

'Beautiful little girl, Mummy's beautiful little girl,' Mrs Armitage cooed. 'Mummy's brought a lovely present for her beautiful baby.' She turned excitedly to Fiona. 'Bring in my small leather travel bag, will you, Fiona? I want to give Mila her present. I hardly knew what to choose. They have such marvellous things in America. Dear little jackets, and wellington boots for her little paws. I could have bought and bought.'

Prinny lowered his ears. He hoped he wasn't going to get any damned fool wellington boots.

Mavis Armitage took a long leather box out of her travel bag and opened it. Lying on velvet was a soft suede collar, intricately shell-edged and finished with a butterfly-shaped buckle studded with bright blue stones. She fastened it lovingly round Prinny's neck.

'There, doesn't she look absolutely gorgeous. It matches her eyes. She must wear it to the cat club show next month.'

Mrs Armitage took her spectacles out of her handbag and put them on her matt-powdered nose. She peered at Prinny.

'Have you been keeping to Princess Mila's high-protein diet sheet?' she asked, frowning. 'She looks a different shape. A bit thinner . . . '

'She's been pining for you,' said Fiona quickly.

'Ah, yes . . . of course, that would explain it. Now my baby must have a nice rest so that she will look beautiful for the cat show.' Prinny sat back on the cushion, speechless. But he would definitely have plenty to say later.

When Mrs Armitage had disappeared upstairs and Prinny was sure the coast was clear, he made his way to Fiona's office and put his paw on her lap. He tilted his head so that Fiona could see the buckle fastening.

'Do you want me to take it off? I thought you wouldn't like it. No, you can't have it to play with. Or bury. Mrs Armitage would be angry. It's probably very valuable. Nor can you sit on my lap, silly. How could I type? And I've got masses to do. Look at all this work she's given me . . . '

But Prinny insisted. He pushed his way on to the chair, sitting behind her like a cushion. He did not particularly like the whine of her electric typewriter, but the flying keys and the fast carriage return were entertaining.

Mrs Armitage was not exactly suspicious, but certain things puzzled her. Princess Mila had always been content to sit on her chair and doze, but now she seemed to have developed a rampant vitality and curiosity, streaking up and down stairs so fast that no one ever really knew where she was. She refused to eat any of her special foods, preferring a helping of whatever Fiona was eating, and her appetite ranged from downright earthy to the quite sophisticated at times.

Princess Mila had never played before, but now she boxed the tassles on the curtains, skidded across the polished floor on the Persian carpet, trampled on the piano keys, and chased everything chaseable, even her own shadow.

And she insisted on telling everyone about it. Mrs

Armitage simply wasn't used to so much vocalising.

'Will you be quiet?' said Mrs Armitage irritably when Prinny was trying to tell her that tea was late. 'I shall shut you in your room if you don't leave me alone. Fiona, for the last half an hour I've been trying to make some telephone calls but Princess insists on pushing in and miaowing down the telephone. My friends can't hear a word I'm saying. You'll have to take her away.'

'Siamese do love to talk,' said Fiona gently.

'Nonsense. Princess never used to be so noisy.'

'Well, Princess was always shut in her room.'

'And that's her place now,' Mrs Armitage snapped, putting on her spectacles and thumbing through her engagement diary.

Fiona carried Prinny away to the kitchen. The cat's cool azure stare told her what he thought of that conversation. He would not be shut in his room, he warned her.

'Please don't be difficult,' she pleaded, swiftly powdering his nose. It was the oddest habit, but one which he had got used to. 'Jobs are hard to find, especially ones with flats, and Mrs Armitage does pay me well.'

But Prinny had a will of iron. He was determined now that he would not go into that room at any cost. He dared Fiona to put him there.

'I said put Princess in her room,' Mrs Armitage called sternly from the hall. 'And I mean now, Fiona.'

Prinny's tail began to whisk. A low growl rumbled in his throat, his ears pricked forward as if stalking, the prey in this case being large, bossy, and, to his eyes, always purple-ribboned.

'Oh dear,' said Fiona, trying to obey.

It was blue murder. It was all hell let loose. Prinny exploded into the most deafening protest of outrage Fiona had ever heard. She stood outside the room with her hands over her ears. She would never have believed that one cat, even a Siamese, could make such a frenzied row.

'I'm going out to Harrods,' said Mrs Armitage, sweeping through the hall with her mink coat over her arm, her face creased with annoyance. 'I trust Princess will have calmed down by the time I return.'

But Prinny had no intention of calming down. The uproar reaching a shattering crescendo . . .

'What on earth is all this racket?'

A man strode into the room – he was tall, solid, dark-browed and unflappable. He scooped Prinny up out of the wreckage of the cushioned bed which he had been violently demolishing. The man held Prinny out at arm's length and gave him a slight shake.

'Stop this fuss at once,' he said firmly, in the kind of voice he used for raw recruits on deck.

A fine cloud of talcum settled on the lapels of his naval coat. Lieutenant Nicholas Armitage looked Prinny straight in the eyes – deep-sea blue met brilliant sapphire blue, and locked instantly.

'This isn't Princess Mila,' said Nicholas to Fiona. 'This Siamese has a wider muzzle, and look at those bright, mischievous eyes. It's younger, slimmer, healthier . . . and male.'

Fiona smiled apprehensively. She put a hand on Prinny's soft cream fur to still the pounding of his heart. He immediately quietened, changed down gear to a lower tone. He was on her side, but he did not know what he could do to help.

'It's a long story . . . '

'I have five days leave.'

'Well, you see, while your aunt was abroad, somehow . . . er . . . somehow I lost Princess Mila,' Fiona confessed. She moistened her lips as she remembered the desperate days that had followed. 'I don't know what happened. I suppose she got out somehow . . . I can't believe she was stolen. Anyway, I reported it to the police, and I went to every home for strays in London, but no Mila. If she had been run over I'm sure someone would have found her and reported it. So I think she must have found herself a new home. But how could I tell your aunt, when she had entrusted Mila to my care? She would have fired me instantly.'

Nicholas agreed. 'She would.'

'Then as it got nearer and nearer to the date of your aunt's return, I was nearly at my wit's end. I decided I would have to find a replacement . . . a look-alike adult Siamese to take Mila's place. And I found Prinny. The markings were so alike . . . '

'But not the character,' said Nicholas, stroking the now-docile cat. Prinny was calmly accepting a new fate. He had met his new master. He loved Fiona, but she was his slave. This man Nicholas was his master.

'Did I do something terribly wrong?' asked Fiona, still stroking the soft fur. 'They told me at the refuge that they would not have kept Prinny much longer. Seven days is usually the maximum, but because he was such a lovely cat. . . ' tears welled into her eyes and Prinny was immediately worried. He patted her cheek sympathetically with his beautiful oval paw. He did not like to see her cry.

'My dear, sweet maiden in distress,' said Nicholas, shifting the cat into her arms, then putting his arms round both of them. 'The solution is at hand. I think it's about time you left my aunt's employment and took on a more interesting and permanent occupation.'

'Prinny's an Australian,' said Fiona incoherently as Nicholas began to kiss her.

'Good on you, sport,' Nicholas drawled.

And good on you, Prinny purred deeply. He did not add pommy-bastard. It would not have been nice.

11 A THOROUGHLY BAD LOT

You only had to take a good long look at Jasper to know that she was a thoroughly bad lot. Her answering glance was always scornful, with only a flicker of interest in the depths of her almond-shaped green eyes. Her long black tail thrashed the ground in perpetual anger. She walked alone. She cared for no one. She refused to conform.

'I don't understand why you're such a bad cat,' said Jennifer. 'You have a good home and you are well fed. And yet you steal. I don't like cats who steal.'

She marched to the back door with Jasper under her arm. She hung there like a limp fur stole, only a minute flick of her tail betraying her inner fury. She did not care if she was not liked. It was quite immaterial to her.

'Stealing Candy's fish, indeed. Ungrateful thing. And it's not the first time I've caught you.' Jennifer tipped Jasper out on to the doorstep. 'Reflect and reform. You can come back when you've repented.'

Repentance. She did not know the meaning of the word. She was uncontrite, even if it was raining. She had not one fleeting whisker of regret. That Candy was going to get exactly what was coming to her.

'Is the delinquent in the stocks again?' asked Edward. 'You know it's raining, don't you? It's not like you to be unkind.'

'I've got to teach her a lesson,' Jennifer insisted, wrestling with her conscience. 'She's been stealing Candy's supper again. Of course, Candy is a perfect lady and won't stand up for herself. Jasper gets away with it every time.'

The perfect lady sat under a chair in a corner of the kitchen, velvet-gold eyes half-veiled, waiting until it was safe to venture out.

'Come on, beautiful,' coaxed Jennifer. 'I've put that bad cat out.'

Candy broke out into a low, passionate purr. Her love was embarrassingly vocal. She could be heard on the telephone, and the mere mention of her name was enough to start the throbbing, quivering, claw-retracting fluffy black Persian on her dauntless track to the nearest soft lap. Nothing deterred Candy in her quest. She was blind to newspapers, sewing, even coffee cups in her way. She would place herself roundly on top of the lot, drooling moist words of love into the nearest ear.

Outside on the windowsill sat Jasper, balefully watching the tender reunion. Although she was nearly full grown, she was still small and sleek – sometimes she thought that one of her ancestors must have been a witch's cat . . . of course, there weren't such things now, what with radar and computers.

The rain settled on her short spiky fur like pearl onions on cocktail sticks. Her attention was caught for a moment by a shining trickling raindrop, and she licked the wet window with a small, inquisitive tongue.

Jasper looked into the kitchen at the bundle of four-inch long Persian fluff now being lovingly brushed and combed by Jennifer, and she felt almost naked by comparison. Electric sparks prickled up her spine. Her tail swung to and fro. She could not stand the nauseating sight any longer.

She jumped down and walked deliberately across a freshly raked flowerbed. Further down the garden tiny shoots of lettuce were peeping through the earth where none had been the day before. She scratched at them curiously and chewed on a tender thread of root.

The bluetits and sparrows were fighting noisily round the bird-bag that swung from the Japanese maple tree. They hung upside down, pecking at the nuts, dropping from a precarious hold, fluttering and squabbling.

Jasper watched them with narrowed eyes. Stupid, irritating things. She could not even be bothered to catch them. She had bigger prey. That long-haired layabout: the precious Candy.

Any good psychiatrist would have sorted Jasper out in a trice. Beneath that smouldering hatred lay a deep-seated inferiority complex; an unconscious distaste for her own black sleekness; a repressed wish for a coat of four-inch long Persian fluff.

Jasper did not understand this. She did not need a motive to be mean – it came naturally. She could not remember a time when she had had a pleasant thought. She had the vaguest memories of a half-wild mother, a crowded cage of stray kittens, of being handled by many strange hands.

Neither did she know that she had been chosen by mistake, nor that she was a profound disappointment to Jennifer. In kittenhood she had looked remarkably like a Persian, and Jennifer had picked her out of the selection at the animal refuge as company for Candy. But it never worked out. The sleeker she grew, the more Jasper disliked the Persian. She brooded for hours on her animosity, plotting horrendously sticky ends for her rival.

'Hello,' said Edward, scooping Jasper up against his shoulder. 'Put you out again, has she? You really will have to learn to behave.'

Jasper reared away from him, back arching, elongating her long neck like a snake. Edward scratched her smooth, almost hairless chin.

'Now you're what I call a real cat,' he said. 'Not like that other overgrown fur mat, all fuzz and fluff.'

Jasper replied with a piercing yeowl and leaped out of his arms. She could not bear all that petting and fuss. Yuck. She shook out her crumpled fur and stalked disdainfully down to the stream.

She trod daintily over the pebbles and thought wicked thoughts. She knew that by engineering something simply terrible for Candy, she would revenge herself on the humans and the pampered Persian at the same time.

She sat on a broken piece of concrete and thought. Death

by drowning was a delicious possibility, but in a mere two inches of slow moving stream? Another tragic road accident – but Candy was as nimble as Jasper in dodging the traffic. Starvation? But the humans were too wily. They had seen through that one.

Jasper thought treacherously of the big golden retriever who lived down the road. Could she, without endangering herself, convince him that Candy, beneath all that fur, was a chewable proposition?

Jasper looked at her own quivering reflection in the shallow water, her eyes darting and flashing among the round pebbles like a shoal of minnows. Perhaps she could get Candy into trouble, then they might get rid of her.

She sauntered back to the house, her tail held high. She watched from the camouflage of a rhododendron bush as Candy was put out of the back door.

'There's a good Candy,' said Jennifer. 'Have a lovely run-round.'

Jasper felt sick. Have a lovely run-round . . . to a cat. It was nauseating.

Candy had a favourite sleeping place. On a rack across the ceiling of the garage were some ladders and Edward had stored the cushions of the garden swing on top of them.

It infuriated Jasper to see Candy up there on her Dunlopillow. It made her deliberately seek out the most uncomfortable box of nails to curl herself up on and go to sleep. She was no softy.

Out of slit eyes Jasper watched Candy go into the garage and climb up the shelves to her throne. She trampled it into order, settled blissfully and began her throbbing vocal appreciation.

Jasper fled down the garden. There must be some way, something that would choke off that awful racket for ever. Her claws caught in some flimsy stuff that was hanging from a shrub. It seemed to have fallen from Jennifer's washing line, and the wind had carried it away. The stuff ripped as Jasper jigged sideways trying to unmesh her claws. She bit and scratched at it, strands catching in her teeth and setting them on edge.

Wildly she leaped about, determined to rid herself of the

hellish stuff. It trailed after her everywhere. She rushed into the garage where there were sharp things and it caught on some logs . . .

Some hours later, when Jasper had almost forgotten the incident, she heard Jennifer saying quite crossly: 'Candy, you naughty thing. Those were my best tights. They're absolutely ruined.'

The days that followed were almost pastoral. Jasper's animosity seemed to mellow into a kind of saintly reserve. She no longer spat at Candy. She deigned to allow Candy her half share of the nourishment provided. She would sit in the same room for several minutes without provoking a squabble.

'I do believe Jasper and Candy are making friends at last,' said Jennifer with relief. 'It's a miracle.'

'Don't be too sure,' said Edward. 'This sudden change of heart doesn't ring true.'

'Jasper's being a good pussy now, aren't you?' Jennifer crooned. 'There's a darling . . . ' The darling good pussy stiffened as Jennifer stroked her sleek black fur. It took immense self-control not to leap out of a window and escape to the woods.

'I think I'll go down to the shops and buy the cats some really nice fish for a treat,' said Jennifer.

'You can go into the newsagents and tell them that the new delivery boy is being highly erratic. And will you pay the gas bill? We've got a final demand. All red print and threats,' said Edward, opening his cheque book. 'You know,' he added thoughtfully, 'perhaps Jasper doesn't like her name. You must admit it sounds very masculine.'

'Nonsense,' said Jennifer. 'It means a kind of quartz, an opaque kind.'

'I know what jasper means, but does she?'

'Or something taking a high polish. Very suitable for a highly-polished cat,' said Jennifer firmly.

'I suppose it doesn't actually make any difference, but I just wondered,' said Edward, signing the cheque with a flourish. 'I suppose it's just a sound to her.'

Jasper remained unmoved. She trod a tightrope of

deception with cool aplomb. She slipped through the waving grasses in the garden, her sharp ears alert for the unexpected. She roamed the area, peering into sheds, nibbling the odd stalk.

The cuddly Candy relaxed into perpetual Elysium; her home was the enchanted fields of Arcadia; the walls vibrated with her ecstatic purring. Her complacency grew with her plumpness.

Jennifer was more surprised than alarmed when one afternoon, she found a uniformed policeman ringing the door bell. He was youngish, fresh-faced and very slightly embarrassed.

'Mrs Jones,' he asked. 'Mrs Edward Jones?'

'That's right,' she said, puzzled.

'I'm making a few inquiries and I'm wondering if you can help me,' he began.

'Yes?'

'We've received a number of complaints in this road about missing items. These complaints cover a period of several weeks. The latest was this morning when a builder working on number 23 reported the loss of a tin of emulsion paint, shade Radiant Blue.'

'I'm afraid I don't understand . . . ' said Jennifer.

'There are paint tracks, shade Radiant Blue, leading into your garage.' The young policeman looked even more embarrassed. 'I wonder if you would allow me to have a look . . . er . . . '

'Of course,' said Jennifer briskly. 'Look all you like. This is absolute nonsense, you know. It was probably some children larking about.'

There were some spots of fresh blue paint on the driveway, and a larger splash by the garage window. Jennifer opened the garage doors, the policeman close behind her. They peered into the gloom. Jennifer switched on the light.

At first all seemed normal. Edward went to work in his car so the garage was empty, apart from the usual flotsam of suburban garages. Jennifer turned to the policeman, triumphantly, but then followed his gaze to the floor. A small pool of Radiant Blue was forming. They looked up at the ceiling, where the drips were coming from.

'Oh dear,' said Jennifer in a small voice, not knowing what to expect next.

The policeman climbed on to the workbench at the end of the garage and reached up among the ladders and cushions from the garden swing. Candy looked down into his youthful eyes and began to purr rapturously, soft fluff a-quiver.

'Oh dear,' said Jennifer again.

'I wonder if you would mind helping me,' he said, sounding quite apologetic.

He passed down the pot of paint, glistening with slopped Radiant Blue. Then he solemnly handed her one child's red wellington boot. Next, three copies of the Radio Times, one unopened gas bill and a dead rose bush. Dried earth showered his uniform.

Jennifer put the items on the floor. 'Is there any more?' she asked hopelessly.

'It's like a jumble sale up here,' he said cheerfully.

The pile on the floor grew . . . a knitted rabbit, a silk scarf from Liberty's, two pairs of bikini panties, one marked Tuesday and the other marked Friday, a man's vest, a brand new pair of secateurs still in their shop packaging. Jennifer went from bright pink with acute embarrassment to pale with horror.

The policeman stretched further into the robber's trove . . . a length of washing line, three odd gloves, a garden trowel, an ordnance survey map of south-west London, a tennis sock and seven pairs of sunglasses.

'I don't understand,' said Jennifer, shaking her head.

'I'm sure there must be some explanation,' the young policeman said.

The explanation sat in the middle of the garden path quickly trying to lick Radiant Blue off her paws. On the path beside her was a carton of yogurt with teeth marks denting the lid and a muddied copy of *Teach Yourself Arabic*.

'Caught red-handed,' said the policeman, almost disbelieving his eyes.

'You mean blue-pawed,' Jennifer remarked, eyeing the cat levelly. 'A serious case of kleptomania.'

Within minutes Jasper was in the kitchen sink up to her middle in warm water, struggling like a demented fiend, as Jennifer tried to wash off the paint before it dried.

'You are a very naughty pussy,' said Jennifer, unable to stop herself from laughing. 'And trying to put the blame on poor Candy. I'm ashamed of you. You're a thoroughly bad lot.'

Jennifer wrapped the cat in a towel. Jasper scowled, knowing she looked a fool with her fur all wet.

'Just you wait until I tell Edward what you've been up to,' said Jennifer, towelling her briskly till her fur shone like silk. Jasper dug her claws into Jennifer's knee. She could not understand what had gone wrong with her plan – they ought to be scolding Candy. She jumped on to the floor and shook off the towel . . . . immediately in her way stood the big black Persian. She met Candy's yellow stare. There was no sympathy in the older cat's knowing eyes. Instead there was a distinctly chilly authority.

Candy sensed a momentary weakening in Jasper's fierce spirit, and stepped forward, a long hiss coming from her curled lips, her fluffy tail hoovering the floor with steady sweeps. She lifted a round velvet paw and boxed Jasper smartly on the ear.

Jasper sprang back, astonished. It hurt.

Jennifer gathered both cats up into her arms, still laughing, and buried her face in their soft fur.

'Now stop it, both of you,' she admonished. 'I won't have any more of this nonsense.'

Jasper veiled her slit eyes and arched her slender neck away from the mass of vibrating Persian almost smothering her. Then she remembered the accuracy of that unexpected wallop, and thought hard. . . perhaps there was room for negotiation after all.

12 THE HONOURABLE MEMBER

Conscious life for this kitten began on the mudflats of the Thames, or rather in a plastic bag on the mudflats. The family had five children to feed on supplementary benefit and a kitten was beyond their means. The man took a 159 bus from Brixton and dropped the plastic bag with the kitten in it over the parapet of Westminster Bridge.

There was no human rescue at hand, for the days of the Roman ford and medieval ferryman had long since vanished into the mists and fog, but the bag floated for a few moments then was caught in the wake of a passing coal barge and washed up on to the mud. With the frantic strength of fear, the kitten tore at the bag, its tiny claws perforating the plastic and pushing through until there was a hole large enough for its head. It wriggled out, its fine baby fluff clinging to it like wet rats-tails.

Unsteadily, trembling, but with a primitive instinct for self-preservation, it negotiated a set of slimy stone steps. It was an alien world, freezing cold, dark and wet. The parapet above loomed gigantic and foreboding; the water below swirled by black and smelly; the evening air curled dank fingers round the helpless creature. It shivered, crawling along endless slabs of pavement, going it knew not where. It squeezed between some tall iron railings that reached to the sky like trees. It found an overturned wire litter basket full of discarded newpapers. The newsprint was warm and nest-like. After licking up fragments of potato crisps from a crumpled bag, the kitten curled into a small ball and went to sleep.

In the morning, the kitten wandered round the outside of the empty building, mewing piteously, but no one saw or heard her. The place seemed to be deserted. She wandered through stone courtyards and cloisters, awed by the grim size of everything towering above her, grey and dingy, flecked with bird droppings, statues crumbling and sinister without faces.

Her nose led her to the kitchen waste. She was too small to eat most of what was there, but a messy slop of cold sago pudding filled her empty stomach till she staggered away, pot-bellied and tired. She found another warm place to sleep, and for the first time a glimmer of hope entered her world.

But the next day she crouched, terrified, in her hiding place. An army had invaded the precincts. Noisy cars, vans, people wearing black shoes and walking with heavy measured treads, rattling trollies laden with crates, clanging bells . . . it was bedlam. Everywhere she crept she was surrounded by hordes of tramping people. Feet appeared from all sides. It was very frightening. She retreated still further into her hiding place. It was only when it began to rain, and the drops bouncing off her tiny nose became a continuous trickle, that she made a wild dash for shelter and found herself indoors.

Now the floor was wood blocks, then a carpeted stairway that went on and on. She climbed the endless green mountain, pausing on each landing to pant and make little lost mewing sounds. Then it was polished wood again and she slid along helter-skelter to the next place, where the carpet was thick and grass-coloured. It was like a great corridor stretching into the distance with high wood-panelled walls; a sensuous warmth oozed from the grills under the dark green padded seats.

Stern portraits gazed down from the walls . . . Sir Marc Brunel, Field Marshal Smuts, Joseph Chamberlain, Sir Isaac Pitman, John Pym, Ramsay Macdonald . . . their eyes followed her, and she gazed innocently back.

The doors to some of the rooms off the corridor were

open. She heard voices coming and hid behind the heavy green curtains. The warmth and darkness were overpowering and she could no longer keep her eyes open. When she awoke all the noise had gone and she could hear herself breathing in the stillness of the night air. Her fluffy coat had dried out and puffed round her like a ginger and white poncho.

She crept out again, with more courage now that she was dry and warm. She found a crumpled ball of paper and patted it curiously. It bounced away from her along a tiled floor and she ran after it, dancing like a wind-blown dandelion clock. The crumpled paper rolled down a wide stone staircase and the kitten bounced after it, sliding and skating on the smooth worn marble, her tiny claws unable to gain a grip of any kind.

She tumbled past marble busts of Gladstone, Palmerston, Pitt, Peel, and Spencer Perceval (the only prime minister to have been assassinated) – their glazed white eyes were unamused. But the fall did not hurt her and at the foot of the staircase she shook out her fur and twitched her small nose. She could smell food, unmistakably. Her flight from the upper regions had brought her near the kitchens . . .

She passed a dining room so vast that she thought she was outside again – the ornate gilt ceiling could have been sun-speckled sky, and the massive portraits in oils on the green-papered walls a landscape of giants.

But there were crumbs under the tables and on an uncleared tray on a side wagon was a small jug of cream. The kitten drank from the Rosenthal bone china and the first small purr of her life throbbed from her throat.

She wandered through the rambling white and chromium kitchens, from one area to another, intoxicated by all the different smells. She would live here in this strange place, she decided, now that she knew where she could always find food. It meant sleeping during the daylight hours when the place was invaded by all those noisy people, and hiding late into the night. But in the small hours until dawn it would be all hers. Long empty corridors to play in, acres of carpets, hundreds of new warm places to curl up in, the creaking of the heating system for company, whispers to chase, ghosts to stalk . . . and as she grew older she discovered that there were mice to catch.

And she had a garden of her own to play in. It was once called the Privy Garden but was now Black Rod's garden, with a small lawn and flowerbeds full of roses. It was easy for her to squeeze through the gaps in the tall iron gates to get there.

Sometimes she wandered along Dirty Lane, an old thoroughfare that now had a more respectable name, and into the Victoria Tower Gardens where Rodin's *Burghers of Calais* stared at her with expressions of grim pity.

There were strange vibrations about the building that puzzled the cat, though she did not know why. The same twelve acres had once been a township and housed many thousands of people – craftsmen, artisans, men-at-arms, cooks and courtiers as well as a royal family. She sensed burning, although she did not know there had been two Great Fires and an air raid on that spot.

She also sensed death and this made her fur prickle. There were echoes of agony in the cobbled courtyard where men had been hung, drawn and quartered and now trees were dying in their concrete beds. More recently there had been the sharp explosion of a bomb near the cloisters, and the acrid fumes clung to the stone.

She loved to stroll in other parts. . . a beautiful red and gilt robing room with priceless furniture and a single high chair that was out of the draughts . . . a long gallery with full-length portraits of quiet, gracious people with dignified faces. But it was the White Hall, or Court of Requests as it had once been called, that she liked best – another lofty room so ornate that it all quite dazzled her. There were three great chairs on a platform with deep red carpeting on the steps – the room was palatial when the moonlight was streaming through the stained glass windows.

Below the three chairs was a wide, rectangular red seat, the cushion of which was stuffed with a blend of commonwealth wool, and the cat found this a very comfortable perch from which to view the magnificence of her surroundings.

She began to learn every corridor, staircase, turret and room. She knew her way over the many different levels of roof, picking a route carefully among gothic spires and unnerving cat-walks to an unexpected small roof garden with abandoned sun-chairs, gay umbrellas and troughs of spilling flowers. She became used to the great clock that periodically erupted into fearsome clanging booms.

As the months passed she grew into a beautiful fluffy burnt-marmalade cat, shading to pale honey, with distinctive white markings on her delicate face. No one ever saw her. Not even the correspondents who worked long after the politicians had gone home, nor the custodians who patrolled the precincts at night, nor the cleaning ladies who came in droves at dawn to vacuum and clear away the litter of discarded paper.

One evening there was a banquet in the vast dining room with the green and white gilded ceiling. A woman came in a long swishing satin dress, rustling and shining with silk embroidery and there were sparkling stones balanced on her head among her hair. Another woman who stayed near her had a halo of fine golden hair and was wearing a long shimmering dress. There were a great many men too, all in black and white, some with sashes and medals, and the room was awash with swishing skirts and small feet in narrow, strappy slippers.

The cat hid under the long table that ran the length of the room by the windows, enclosed by curtains of starched white table linen. She could see all the feet, the gold and silver sandals, the shiny black shoes. Toes twitched, and some people eased their feet out of their shoes as the meal went on; sometimes a hand slipped down to scratch an ankle or pull up a black silk sock.

Crumbs came her way but she was not interested in crumbs these days. The smoked salmon people were eating was rarely dropped, but they were not very hungry, and she knew that there would be the usual mountains of delicious scraps shovelled into the waste bins for her to turn over at her leisure.

The evening dragged on, and the clattering dishes and cutlery mingled with the drone of voices in conversation eventually drove her to sleep. She woke up with a start when simultaneously all the chairs were scraped back and everyone stood up, some searching surreptitiously for their shoes. A great shout went up: 'The Queen! The Queen! God bless her.'

The cat ate too well after the banquet and fell asleep at once in her favourite hiding place. It was on a foot-shelf at the back of a huge, heavy square table with claw legs and drawers, standing in front of a baronial fireplace in the Upper Waiting Hall. Someone else had once liked this foot-shelf for it was deeply scored with spur marks from a man's boots.

She always sensed burning here too. Perhaps the great table had been saved from some horrendous fire, or perhaps it was just the smell of soot that still clung to the crooked chimney above the now unused fireplace.

She slept too long and too deeply. It was quite the wrong place to be caught in daylight. When she heard the cleaning ladies arriving with their pails and mops, she fled down into the central lobby, caught again by the barrenness of the high vaulted octagonal hall with nowhere secret to hide. The statues of medieval kings and queens stood impassively in their niches in the walls, as she crept under a long dark green leather seat, curling her tail tightly round her, freezing into immobility.

''Ere, Ethel, I thought I saw a cat.'

'Don't be silly. You're dreaming. There's no cat here. Ought to be though . . . there's enough mice about.'

The floor was cold stone though not far away was an iron grill through which wafted warm air. A statue of Queen Charlotte, sad and beautiful, loomed above; a squat red fire extinguisher sat below.

She had chosen quite the wrong place to hide, because it became very busy indeed. A queue of people constantly formed and reformed at a window, saying things like 'Four first-class and eleven second-class please,' and 'How much is a postcard to the States?' She could not get any sleep at all because of the comings and goings. People sat on her seat, waiting for their name to be called, and her tail was in constant danger of being trodden on.

Crowds surged through the lobby – tourists, delegations, policemen, parties of schoolchildren. She had never seen so many people at once. Then a policeman began to clear back the sightseers, and in solemn silence a procession marched through the lobby with men in black gowns, black breeches, one in silver-buckled shoes, another who seemed to have some sort of authority was carrying a heavy golden club. They walked through the people, along a picture-lined corridor towards the other chamber with the green hide seats and high oak galleries.

She followed curiously, unnoticed for once in all the commotion, sliding along the walls in the wake of the procession.

Never before had she seen this man with the silver buckles on his shoes and the long woolly grey hair. He looked nice, she thought, friendly and approachable. She had never approached a human being.

The procession went into the green chamber and the golden club was deposited on a pair of brackets on the table. The man with the buckles climbed into a high, canopied chair at the north end of the chamber beyond the table and put his feet on a green leather footstool. On the table were two brass-bound despatch boxes, and several heavy books, pens and stationery.

She crept under a bench at the back and made herself as small as possible. A pair of brown suede shoes shuffled a twitch away from her whiskers. There was a great deal of standing up and sitting down again. She could not understand this unusual form of exercise.

What began as a reasonable sort of exchange of views began to get noisy. Voices got louder. No one seemed to be listening to anyone else. There was shouting and interjections, unruly jeering and bursts of raucous laughter.

'If these figures are true and I do not doubt for one moment that they are, then why does not the right honourable lady admit that her policy is a ghastly failure?' a voice boomed across the floor, the microphone picking up the righteous indignation of his tone.

A wave of objections and counter-cheering almost drowned the lady's reply.

'It is not for politicians to try to take over the management of public sector industries,' insisted a cool voice.

Members sprang to their feet, waving order papers. The uproar grew. No one could hear a word.

'What price the election now?' someone shouted above the clamour.

'Point of Order, Mr Speaker. Point of Order!'

'Order! Order!' thundered the man in the tall, canopied chair, trying to make himself heard over the din. But the pandemonium grew as more Members rose to their feet, insisting on being heard, arguing across the floor of the House, encouraged by their jeering colleagues.

'Order! Order!'

The cat was terrified, deafened by the noise, her fur standing on end. Some unspeakable calamity was obviously imminent. A third Great Fire? An explosion? Were the massive stone walls about to descend on their heads, crushing them all to death?

In sheer panic, she shot across the floor of the House. But there was no immediate way out. She leaped on to the table, scattering papers in all directions; knocking over a jug of water. Her claws sank into the oak of the canopied chair and she streaked upwards, almost reaching the dusty top. The parliamentary correspondents leaned over from the Press Gallery, refreshed by the diversion.

'My goodness,' said Mr Speaker. 'Catch that cat!'

But no one could catch her. Not the Members, nor the Clerks, nor the official doorkeepers with their silver chains of office, nor the dignified Sergeant-at-Arms who was supposed to apprehend all unwanted strangers and escort them to the Carriage Gates or to the first floor detention room in the clock tower.

Then someone had the sense to open wide the heavy brass-studded carved oak doors behind the Speaker's Chair, and catching sight of an exit, the cat slithered down and fled to freedom.

News of the marmalade cat spread faster round the Palace of Westminster than an election rumour. Everyone quite liked the idea. It made the gothic mound more human.

She found that she no longer had to hide during the day and only surface in the lonely hours of the night. As she wandered around, people stopped to say hello, to give her a stroke or scratch her ears. There were several secretaries who encouraged her to visit them and to watch them typing on top quality cream-coloured paper then share their coffee breaks; the librarians were pleased that she kept the mice away from their precious old volumes and records of Hansard; more than one waitress would save an odd slice of chicken or a few prawns in case they saw her.

And you might see her too. Perhaps one day when you are sitting in the Public Gallery listening to a debate, you might catch a glimpse of a fluffy ginger and white tail under the Speaker's Chair. On the other hand, it might just be a trick of the light.

13 CHIMNEYS

It was a blustery November day when we drove down to Surrey – the wild wet leaves hurled themselves against the windscreen and fouled up the wipers. Jenny and I were going to Chimneys, outside the village of Lambhurst, to look after Aunt Polly's house while she was away in Florida for a month.

It was an arrangement which was convenient to us all. Our North London flat was being pulled apart while workmen put in a new central heating system, and I was only too happy to leave my landlord to sort out all the problems and clear up the mess.

Aunt Polly, like many house owners these days, had a fear of squatters, and was loath to leave her house empty for so long. Jenny was recovering from a bad bout of measles and the doctor agreed that a few weeks running free in Surrey would probably do her more good than a hasty return to school.

'Besides, one of those weeks is half term,' Jenny told Dr Stuart, sitting up in bed, her long fringe spiking her lashes. 'So I really shan't be missing that much.'

'Don't worry,' I said firmly. 'I shall be taking your school books with us to Chimneys so that you can start catching up, young lady.'

Jenny pulled a sweet, pert face. She was tall for her age, with Stephen's candid brown eyes and my silky dark hair, still pallid from her illness but already restless and fidgety with sudden surges of new energy.

'Aunt Polly's new house is lovely,' said Jenny, turning to Dr Stuart with enthusiasm. 'You must come and see it. We went there once last summer for tea and had raspberries picked from the garden.'

'Perhaps your mother won't want to be bothered with visitors,' said Andrew Stuart, packing his stethoscope away in his slim, executive version of a doctor's black bag. 'She could do with a rest as well. You are both too pale and skinny for my liking.'

'Oh, Mummy, did you hear that?' said Jenny cheekily. 'Dr Stuart thinks that all women should be pink and fat.'

Dr Stuart was new to the group practice and certainly Jenny had become very friendly with him during her illness. Perhaps it was not surprising, because there was no man in our life. Ours was a one-parent family.

I went cold, even now, six years later, whenever I thought of my handsome Stephen's death in a mid-air aeroplane collision over Tokyo. What could have gone through his mind in that moment, that split second of knowledge before the disaster? I could only hope that there had been no moment, that he had been engrossed in the paperback thriller I had bought him at the airport bookstall; or perhaps he had been dozing on the long flight and the whole event had been no more than a slipping into a deeper, lasting sleep.

Dr Stuart had come into our lives along with Jenny's spots and he had been a reliable guide through the worst days of her fever. He was in his early thirties, often bone weary, but with disarming laughter crinkles round his deep set eyes which could chase away the weariness. He looked as if he could do with a month at Chimneys.

'Of course we should be pleased to see you,' I said. 'Anytime.'

'Thank you,' he said. 'That's very kind.'

Chimneys stood behind a high stone wall outside the village near woods, draped in trees like a house in a fairy tale. As we drove along the lane that skirted the wall we could see the top half of the long, rambling, mellow red-brick building with its odd, disjointed roof slopes and small, square, lattice-paned windows that glinted in the watery late afternoon sunlight.

'Oh, Mummy,' said Jenny, clutching my arm with sudden excitement. 'It's going to be lovely here, I know it is.'

Aunt Polly had found the house on one of her erratic car-wandering Sundays, and fortunately she could afford to buy it. In her youth Aunt Polly had wandered a lot further afield than Surrey, sometimes dressed as a man, sometimes only with an Arab guide, and her travel books had brought her a steady income ever since.

'Mind you, they're old hat these days,' she was fond of saying. 'It's package tours everywhere. There's nowhere left to explore. It's such a shame.'

We drove past a small, narrow door set in the stone wall, its wood warped and weatherbeaten, the brick supports and overhead archway listing dangerously. I smiled to myself. I liked to think of all the slippings-in and out that might have occurred through that convenient little exit.

'Here we are,' I said, driving into the courtyard.

The beginnings of Chimneys went back to Elizabethan times when a wealthy and perhaps titled family decided to have a small hunting lodge in which to eat and rest after a tiring day's hunting over the North Downs, or in which to spend a month in the country away from London's pollution or plague.

Instead of the usual timbered Tudor style, they built a cosy tile-hung, double fronted lodge with four angular bay windows and a great central chimney.

The rooms were of unusually pleasant proportions; the ceilings ranged from low, black beams to delicate, high, scrolled plasterwork; every room had a wealth of oak joinery and panelling; a wide oak staircase was lightened by an eight-foot, coloured glass window with a golden winged horse and the inscription *confido conquiesco*; then the staircase narrowed, twisting and turning its way up into a warren of little rooms in the roof.

The gem of the lodge was an original hand-painted stained glass window set into an internal wall. It did not belong to any room so one could only guess where it might have been in the original structure. Now it was part of the hall and the centre panel opened out on to the modern kitchen with washing machine and working tops, a far different view from the rolling Surrey hills it must once have overlooked.

The window was nearly four feet square, the upper three panels half the size of the lower three. Each had an exquisitely hand-painted scene – an Elizabethan huntsman, in velvet coat and plumed hat, seated on a heavy-chested, pawing horse; a demurely-dressed woman offered a jug of refreshment to a seated rider; another woman waited alone with a small spaniel at her feet – the painting was delicate and fine, the colours still as fresh as if they had been painted yesterday.

Each scene was set into small rectangular amber panes, each glowing with captured sunlight; then round the outside of each of the six panes was a row of clear bottle-top shaped glass, the blunt broken-off stalk of each round piece of glass now worn smooth and harmless by time. I could pass my hand over the entire structure without fear of a scratch or a nick.

'Oh, Mummy, it all looks like necklaces,' Jenny had said, the first time she had seen the window. 'So pretty, like big glass necklaces for horses or cows.'

She ran straight to the window as we let ourselves into the oak-beamed hall.

'It's still here,' she cried, laying her cheek momentarily against the cold glass. 'Oh, Mummy, I love it . . . '

'Of course it's still here,' I said, carrying in our cases and a basket of shopping. Aunt Polly would probably have left a full refrigerator but then she might have turned it off in the flurry of her departure to the States.

At some point in time the original kitchen and outhouses had been pulled down to make way for an elegant high-ceilinged Regency extension to the south of the lodge. The thirty-foot-long drawing-room had a high, wood-panelled ceiling, square lattice-paned windows with cosy window-seats and a massive fireplace to take huge Surrey logs. The long bedroom above had another such fireplace to take off the chill. Other additions were three chimneys and a timbered bell tower with a sweet sounding brass bell to summon wanderers to their meals or remind them that dusk was imminent and it was no longer safe to roam the Surrey lanes.

Much later a Victorian family took over the house, seeking the unsullied country air for their growing family of children. On the other side of the hunting lodge they built another extension in mock Gothic, adding the necessary enormous kitchen, a large, square, tiled dining hall with the five angels of war represented on one set of stained glass windows and the five angels of peace on another. The doors had gothic arches and carved over the stone fireplace was the motto *Virtute et fide vinco* – 'By virtue and faith I win'. With all those angels, such an awesome inscription and a bell to summon them to church, I felt the Victorian family must have been models of propriety. And they added two more chimneys.

When Aunt Polly found the house it had been owned by two sisters for years. They had lived in a couple of rooms and the rest were shut up and neglected. A builder wanted to pull it down, already having parcelled off most of the extensive grounds for a modern housing estate.

However, he had reckoned without Aunt Polly. She had lovingly restored the place, modernised the kitchen and bathrooms, put in central heating, and removed various monstrous 'improvements' so that each part of the house was as near to the original as possible.

'Don't tell me it's too big for me,' Aunt Polly said defiantly whenever she caught that look in someone's eye. 'They won't get me to move. So they needn't even try. I like space. I couldn't live in a pokey place.'

Our North London flat was certainly a pokey place by comparison and another reason why Aunt Polly's invitation had been so welcome.

'I want you to look after all my plants while I'm away,' she said over the telephone. 'I could get someone from the village to come in, but they might forget. And I've one or two rather delicate specimens.'

I guessed that might be an understatement. It was. The conservatory was a semi-jungle. I could see I was going to spend half my time indoor gardening.

Jenny immediately threw off all lingering effects of measles and took to the woods. From the kitchen window I could keep track of her bright red anorak as she ran and skipped, exploring the walled garden and the wild land beyond.

'Aunt Polly's got the sweetest little cat,' said Jenny, bursting into the kitchen, her cheeks rosy from running.

'I didn't know Aunt Polly had a cat,' I said. 'She didn't mention it to me. Only her plants . . . '

'I expect she forgot because she's getting old,' said Jenny, well aware of my poor memory. 'But we will look after her, won't we, Mummy?'

'Of course we will. I'll buy some cat food when we go into the village.'

'Can I go and play with Mopsie until tea is ready?'

'Mopsie? Is that what you are going to call her? What a funny name!'

But Jenny was quite firm about it. 'Oh no, she likes the name. When I told her, she looked pleased. She looks just like she's made of tinsel, Mummy. All Christmassy.'

I had to laugh. 'A tinsel cat?'

'She's so pretty, almost white but sort of tipped with red, like tinsel. And she had lovely turquoise eyes.'

Jenny did not play outside for long as the November evening darkened suddenly, and she came scurrying indoors for hot crumpets toasted in front of the fire, smothered with butter that dripped between her fingers. She sat in front of the log fire, licking her fingers, mesmerised by the flickering shadows cast by the flames. She looked better already. I felt some of the tension ease out of my neck and shoulders – I was always so frightened when she was ill. I could not bear to lose her as well.

It seemed a bit ridiculous standing outside calling 'Mopsie' so I compromised with the universally-understood 'Puss . . . puss,' wondering if the cat missed the warmth of Aunt Polly's fireside and the old lady's flow of chatter. The cat did not come. Perhaps she had a hideaway in the unused stables or the garages.

But obviously the cat knew some secret way in and out of the house because most nights she slept on Jenny's bed.

'She's lovely and warm,' said Jenny. 'I can feel her weight. Then if I wake up, I can hear her purring.'

The wind seemed to drive Mopsie wild. I could hear Jenny laughing as she chased after the cat all over the house.

'Mopsie? Where are you now?' Jenny scampered up the narrow staircase to the attic bedrooms. 'Are you polishing the floor with your tail, Mopsie? Whoops! Off we go again . . .'

Jenny came flying into the kitchen and went straight to the tap for a drink of water. 'Oh, Mopsie's been so funny this morning! I think she was chasing the wind! Sliding and leaping all over the place. Eventually she jumped on to a window seat and I had to let her out. She danced away across the lawn, playing with the leaves, her fur all sparkling.'

'I know,' I nodded. 'The wind does something to some cats. Perhaps it affects their acute hearing.'

Mopsie never came into the kitchen for anything to eat. The catfood in the dish went stale and I had to throw it away. Nor did she touch any of the milk I put down.

'She hunts,' explained Jenny. 'She catches all her own food. And she drinks water. I've seen her lapping at a little puddle.'

So I gave up worrying about feeding her. Cats can always look after themselves and this one seemed to have adopted a more nomadic life while her mistress was away.

'Mummy, she's sitting on the stairs looking just like one of those big china cats. Come on, Mopsie, let's go and explore . . .'

I heard the back door close as the pair of them went out. Mopsie kept out of my way. Perhaps she did not trust strange adults. Perhaps she only liked children and mildly eccentric old ladies.

I spoke to Dr Stuart on the telephone and he agreed that Jenny did not need her prescription renewed. Her appetite had returned and she was once again the energetic little girl she had been before the measles. In fact I wished she would spend more time with her books, but she seemed so happy chasing about the garden and woods that I let her be.

'Don't worry,' said Dr Stuart. 'She's an intelligent child. She'll soon catch up.'

'I wish I shared your confidence,' I said. 'It's these eleven-plus exams. It's not right that children so young should be put under such pressure.'

'Then don't put on the pressure,' he said. 'Jenny will find her own level.'

But every evening I made sure that Jenny did spend some time reading her school books and writing some of the exercises which her teacher had set. While she worked quietly in front of the fire, I sewed or knitted, making new clothes for Jenny's return to school. We always sat in the Elizabethan room for it was smaller to heat, and we both loved the pretty, ornate ceiling. When my eyes were tired from sewing it was so restful to gaze at the delicate roses and sprays of wild blackberries with which those craftsmen had decorated the ceiling so long ago.

Jenny let out a long, exaggerated sigh as she chewed the end of her pencil.

'I'm not surprised you're finding it difficult,' I said a little primly. 'You spend all day playing when you should be working.'

Jenny snuggled back against my knees. I pushed my finger through her silky hair. How lucky I was to have this precious child.

'But we've had such a lovely day,' she yawned. 'Mopsie and I found a frog. It really made me jump, but Mopsie wasn't frightened at all. She's not frightened of anything.'

I smiled and gave her a little push. 'You obviously don't intend to do any more work, young monkey. You'd better go and have your bath.'

I opened the heavy velvet curtains and sat in a deep leather armchair by the window, watching the ferocious wind whipping the last of the garden leaves in the semi-darkness. The withered leaves flattened themselves against the little panes of glass, only to be whisked away by the next gust. I switched off the table lamp, enjoying the leaping shadows from the fireplace.

Something brushed my leg and I looked down. A beautiful pale cream, almost white cat was padding silently across the carpet. The fur on her head, back and tail was delicately tipped with red, the colour of a cameo. As she moved the fur rippled and sparkled in the firelight, catching the glow, yet the light shone through the fine furry coat making her beauty almost ethereal. The cat turned and looked at me. She had the strangest eyes, almost emerald or blue-green, a kind of luminous turquoise. She had an air of quiet dignity, an expression of sweet repose. I could understand why Jenny loved her.

'Why, hello Mopsie,' I said, for it could only be her. 'So we meet at last. Will you come and say hello to me?'

I held out my hand and moved forward to stroke the cat or perhaps just to see if she would let me touch her. At the very instant I moved there was a fearful crash and the window in front of which I had been sitting shattered into a thousand pieces. Long slivers of glass pierced the chair, the arrow-like shafts slicing through the leather.

A huge branch swayed against the window, brittle grey branches poking through the lattice. The wind had torn a limb from the dead elm at the far wall and hurled it against the window.

I knelt on the floor, shaking, as the glass settled with twinkling fairy-like sounds. I broke out into a clammy sweat. I could have been cut to ribbons. If I had not moved towards the cat, the glass would have torn through my flesh as swiftly as it had ripped the leather of the chair.

Mopsie had vanished, frightened probably by the noise of the falling glass.

When I collected my senses, I put on some kitchen gloves, fetched a dustpan and brush and began clearing up the glass. It took a long time. I searched the carpet thoroughly for fragments which might injure the cat's paws. Aunt Polly had mentioned the dead elm; some tree-loppers were due to come and take it down. It had stood like a stark grey skeleton for over a year. I dragged the chair back into an alcove; it would have to be re-covered.

Jenny came down in her dressing-gown, her face pink from her bath. 'Whatever happened?' she asked, her eyes round. 'I heard the most awful crash.'

'A branch of the dead elm crashed against the window. Don't come in here without any slippers on. I have cleared it up but it's so easy to miss a little piece of glass. It gets everywhere, so be careful, won't you? By the way, I saw Mopsie.'

'Gosh, what a mess.' Jenny seemed more interested in the broken window. 'Oh, did you?'

'She's a very pretty cat.'

'I told you she was. Can I have some milk and biscuits? I've had my bath and I've washed and dried my hair.'

'All right, but have it in bed. I think it would be better if we did not use this room until I've had a chance to clear up again in daylight.' I drew the curtains across the broken window and dampened down the fire.

Before I went to bed I searched the house for Mopsie, but she had gone out her own secret way, and as I closed the front door I thought I saw a shadow streak through the distant trees.

Andrew Stuart came down the following weekend and we all went on a long, muddy trudge along the ridge of the hills. He seemed quite different in old corduroys, a thick jersey under his anorak and a tweed cap pulled down against the stinging rain. He was delighted by Jenny's recovery. She had more energy than either of us and covered twice the ground, dashing off at tangents to explore. We walked more steadily, discovering things that we liked talking about.

'I thought you would be bringing a wife and a car full of kids,' I said, as we turned for home. 'I've made a mountain of rock cakes.'

We laughed at my silly joke and he said; 'I've never had time to meet anyone. A GP's social round is somewhat limited, unless you happen to fall for a nurse. And I didn't.'

He was standing in the hallway taking off his muddy boots when he noticed the tall stained glass window, the coloured glass lighting up the opposite wall with a kaleidoscope of pastel pinks and greens.

'Confido conquiesco,' he said, reading the inscription

under the winged horse. 'My Latin is a bit rusty but I think that means "I believe in being still . . . in taking rest, in repose, in quiet. I believe firmly . . ." ' he went on, almost to himself.

His words found a response in myself. I had seemed so much more contented these past few days, more relaxed, as if the long, heavy burden of grief I had put upon myself was beginning to ease. Perhaps my own miraculous escape from injury and disfigurement had something to do with it.

'Take care of yourself,' said Andrew, touching my hand. The touch was half professional, and half something quite different.

Aunt Polly returned from America with a Florida tan and armfuls of gift-wrapped surprises for us. Everything over there was 'wonderful' and she was full of plans for returning next autumn.

'And sometime I'll take you with me, young lady,' she said, pulling Jenny to her. 'If you are a good girl with your school work and pass all your O-levels and B-levels, or whatever they call them these days.'

'She won't do that here,' I said drily. 'Her concentration has only been a few degrees above nil. She has spent all her time playing with your cat.'

Aunt Polly was taking off her hat and fluffing out her tinted hair. She paused before she answered. 'Oh?'

'I'm afraid we didn't know her real name, so we've been calling her Mopsie,' I went on.

'One name's as good as another,' said Aunt Polly enigmatically.

When it was time for us to go and the car was packed up with our luggage and a bunch of late chrysanthemums from the garden Jenny detached herself from us and wandered away. For a moment she stood by the little door in the wall as if she were listening.

'I'm just going to say goodbye to Mopsie,' she said. There was a little quiver in her voice and I ached for her. She was too young to begin sad partings.

She ran off and we saw her disappear into the trees.

'My dear, before you go, I must tell you something.' Aunt Polly's tone was troubled. 'I don't have a cat.'

I didn't understand. 'Oh yes, you have,' I said.

'The only cat in this house is the one in the hall,' she said strangely. I followed her back into the house. We were in the Elizabethan hunting lodge, the oldest part, where the unusual stained glass window now opened out on to the modern kitchen area. I had passed it a hundred times a day, always with a glance of admiration for its glowing brilliance.

'Look carefully at the hunting scene,' said Aunt Polly. It was the largest of the painted scenes, showing the hunt in full flight, a leaping deer followed by sturdy horses and lean hounds caught in mid-bark.

Aunt Polly drew my gaze to the lower left-hand corner of the scene where a small crack had been repaired with leading. Watching the huntsmen from a safe and secret hiding-place was a creamy, almost white cat painted with the finest streaks of red tipping its fur; a cat with eyes the colour of bright turquoise. She glowed in the painting, like a cameo.

I said nothing. What could I say? I remembered the way Jenny had embraced the glass on our arrival. I touched the cold painting lightly with the tips of my fingers. I was trying to say thank you to Mopsie.

Some weeks later Andrew brought Jenny a kitten. She had been abandoned in a dustbin by some youths. She was a daft little thing – a tabby with pretty silver streaks. Jenny called her Moppety.

When the wind blew Moppety went wild. She would dash all over the flat, her small paws skating on the polished floors sending mats a-flying, curtains flapping. I could hear Jenny laughing as she scrambled after her kitten.

Moppety would eventually scratch at a window to be let out on to the balcony. Then, with one carefree glance back, she would dance away, chasing the scurrying dust, knocking over flower pots, her feathery tail held high like a sparkling plume.

14 A FAMILY AFFAIR

It was a confusing family at first sight. There was the father, the mother and their son, and the mother's sister. The two sisters originally lived together; the father and son had at one time lived together. But now, through force of circumstances, the whole family was under one roof.

The two sisters were inseparable. They sat close together at the top of the stairs like book-ends, or curled up under a table, lovingly entwined so that it was hard to tell who was who. If one were ill, they both had to be taken to the vet. If one wanted to go out into the garden, they both went out. It was the same with coming in.

They were a family of Colourpoints. Beautiful, exotic creatures of extravagant Persian fluff, with the delicate colouring of a Siamese, intelligent minds and gentle ways.

Cy, the father, was a massive Blue Colourpoint. But he was not a blue cat, he was a grey cat. He had an unmistakably masculine, butch face and a withdrawn nature. He did not make friends easily, but preferred to watch and contemplate. No one ventured to cuddle him. Any such familiarity would have been an offence to his patriarchal dignity. And he was huge, an enormous platter of a cat who could overwhelm any rash admiration by slow suffocation.

His mate, Chien, a Seal Colourpoint, was a pale brown beauty; she was the Vivien Leigh of the family. Delicate, well-bred, utterly enchanting . . . and yet, beneath all that beauty lurked an anatomical abnormality: her birth canal was too narrow, and her kittens did not survive. She bore one dead one after another, so Eleanor had her spayed. Chien wore her newly enforced sterility with a gentle sadness.

Fu, the only one of her kittens to survive, was a rich Chocolate Colourpoint – a male cat of outstanding handsomeness, loving and curious, an open generous nature and an air of courage. He was like a young knight, fearless and ready for life, knowing that one day he would sire a great strain of champions. But meanwhile there was the world to enjoy and explore . . .

The odd one out was Cheynne (pronounced Shay-knee), the sister-in-law of Cy, sister of Chien, aunt of Fu. She was the odd one out in every way, but most particularly in her colouring. She was that rare creature, a Tortie Colourpoint. Nature had got her brushes in a twist when dabbing the paint on Cheynne. Her face was unbelievable. At first the blotches of colour seemed to obscure all features. But gradually the patches of black, brown, red, tan and white took on shape and meaning, and a sweet, enigmatic face emerged from the blobs.

She behaved somewhat like a maiden aunt, too. She rarely approached her brother-in-law, thinking that such fraternisation might be unseemly. She occasionally crossed the path of her adventurous nephew, remembering that the family tie needed to be knotted at times. But she preferred to spend her days clinging to her sister's side like a mottled shadow, as if waiting for some of her sister's beauty to transfer itself to her.

Now that all four cats were living together it was perfect for them, confusing for visitors and expensive for Eleanor. When Cy and Fu's original owner had to go abroad, it had seemed a practical solution of what to do with the cats. Also, Eleanor hoped that the presence of Chien's husband and son would bring the young mother out of her post-operation blues.

But Cy made no move towards his wife or anyone else. He sat remotely, usually on a high point, watching the world, like some vast grey bolster. He did not even come for his food when Eleanor put it down, but waited until she had retired from the kitchen before heaving himself from aloft and stalking across the floor.

Fu was the perfect guest, amusing and friendly, making himself at home, being deferential to his mother and his aunt. Eleanor's large garden was a delight and when it snowed he leaped out, playing with the snowflakes and tumbling about in drifts like a child.

The cats were, in many ways, like her children. Eleanor had long passed the age when most of her friends had married. She thought quite calmly that it was unlikely she would ever marry now, and it did not worry her. Her parents had left her a house to live in, and in fact her life held many compensations. She could please herself, whatever she wanted to do. She could cook, or not cook. She never had to wash dirty socks, pants or shirts. She never had to clean up after muddy manly feet. And apart from her responsibility towards the cats, she could come and go as she pleased. It was a freedom she would not give up lightly . . . .

And it was just as well she did not have a husband to look after when it took over half an hour every day to groom the cats. Cy stood, as rigid as a sentry on duty, enduring her administrations stoically. Fu thought it was an extension of playtime and the brush was the prize. Chien and Cheynne behaved exquisitely as if esconced in an expensive beauty salon.

When it was time for Chien's stitches to come out, Eleanor put the two sisters in their cat box on to the front passenger seat in the car. The box was not really big enough for two cats but they were used to this mode of travel and curled round each other, noses poking through the fluff for air.

Eleanor thought Chien was still off-colour so she drove extra carefully to cause the least distress to her passengers. It worried her that Chien was unwell. She remembered how Chien's eyes had tried to tell her something during the long, difficult birth of her last dead kittens. Eleanor had felt so helpless. Now, at least, the cat would not have to go through that agony again.

There were so many ruts in the road – the council seemed

to be forever digging it up for one reason or another. Eleanor slowed down as she saw new roadworks ahead and a red light halting her lane of traffic.

When the light turned to green, everything else moved except Eleanor. Her car stalled. Again and again she tried to bring the engine to life, but it only turned over with a dull whine.

'Hell,' she said, and got out of the car to see what was the trouble.

'I sympathise profoundly. An embarrasing situation for the liberated female drivers of today, unless, of course, you really do know what goes on inside that car bonnet?'

Eleanor turned to the speaker. She met the granite-grey eyes of the most attractive man she had seen for years. He was sitting at the wheel of a dark E-type Jaguar, regarding her with amusement, an aura of success on his well-built shoulders as surely as if he had his bank balance clocking up on the veneered dashboard.

'I must confess, I don't. I was hopefully going through the motions. There might be a loose wire or something . . .'

'What innocence! Let me have a look,' he said. He swung his car off the road and climbed out without opening the door. He poked around the innards of Eleanor's old Hillman, tried the ignition again, then got out of the driver's seat, wiping his hands on a spotless silk handkerchief.

'You've run out of petrol,' he said.

'Hell,' said Eleanor again.

'Can I telephone your husband for you? Perhaps he could come and collect you?'

'No husband,' said Eleanor. 'Don't worry, I can manage.' She lifted the cat box out of the car and locked the doors.

'What are you going to do?' he asked.

'Walk,' she said. 'I'll come back later with a can of petrol. Thank you for your help.'

'Have you got far to go?'

'It's about a mile and a half.'

'Hop in. I'll take you. It's no trouble. Let me put your

box in the boot.'

'How kind, thank you. But I'll keep this on my knee – it's a cat box.'

She felt the man beside her almost stifle a shudder. There was a slight pause as he concentrated on moving the low car out into the traffic.

'You'll forgive me if I don't go into raptures and say nice pussy,' said the man with some apprehension. 'But I suffer from ailurophobia – a fear of cats – like the great Napoleon.'

'Perhaps I'd better get out,' said Eleanor. 'I have two cats with me.'

'I shall be all right,' he said, looking straight ahead, 'as long as I don't hear them, see them or smell 'em.'

'They don't smell,' said Eleanor quickly.

'Right, then let's talk about something else.' He started telling Eleanor about himself, and she wondered how anyone could be afraid of cats. Was it their fur that set teeth on edge? Or the stealthy way they walked, or the unfathomable inscrutability of their eyes? She could not ask him.

His name was Bruce Levant. He worked with a record publishing company and travelled extensively promoting new groups. It all sounded very glamorous, moving in a circle of pop stars, flying to New York and Las Vegas, golden and platinum discs, million dollar sales . . . a far cry from teaching in a girls' private school and living in the same house all her life with four Colourpoint cats.

A week later Eleanor was shooing the four cats into her bedroom. Cy was reluctant to leave his perch on the dresser and she had to carry him, heavyweight that he was, upstairs.

'I'm very sorry,' she said, slightly out of breath. 'I know you think this is undignified but I've got a visitor coming. And although he's very nice in every way, he just doesn't take to cats.' They regarded her with offended eyes. Chien, who had still not fully recovered her spirits, looked both pained and hurt. Fu decided to make the best of a poor show and jumped on Eleanor's bed with a look of defiance.

'Okay,' said Eleanor, giving in. 'You can go on my bed, just this once. But don't make a habit of it.'

They would not have done, except that Bruce began to make a habit of visiting Eleanor. She simply could not understand it. She was six years older than him. He was devastatingly attractive, whereas she . . . well, she had always thought of herself as very ordinary, although now she noticed a glow in her cheeks, a sparkle in her eyes. She lightened the shade of her hair with a minky-coloured tint, darkened her long pale lashes with mascara. And she bought some new clothes, willowy and thin, all quite useless for school.

'Because you are different,' said Bruce, when she asked him why he wanted to see her again. 'You are so refreshing. All these pop singers, punk stars, groupies . . . my dear, if only you could see yourself beside them. Then you would know why I am falling in love with you.'

Eleanor's heart lurched. She could hear her own heartbeats. It was all too soon . . . and wonderful. She was afraid to let herself fall in love. After all these years? How could she really believe that this was happening, and with someone like Bruce?

'Stop pretending you're a little mouse,' he teased. 'Have a look in the mirror. Has no one ever told you that your eyes are the colour of pansies? So blue and velvety, and so shy and demure.'

'I'd better go and make some coffee,' said Eleanor briskly, 'before you make any more silly remarks.'

'Fine, I'm all for some coffee,' he chuckled. He turned the lights down and leafed through her records for some soft music. 'But I warn you, I'm about to make a lot of silly remarks . . .'

Later that evening, much later, as she heard the low throb of Bruce's car driving away, Eleanor drifted up to her bedroom and found all four cats curled up on her bed in a great heap. They blinked at the sudden light and Chien sneezed.

She sat on the edge of the bed, stroking them absent-mindedly in a circular movement that encompassed all four.

'What on earth am I going to do?' she asked them. 'He can't live with you, and I think I can't live without him.'

But it was a problem she happily shelved. The girls at school whispered among themselves, 'Miss is in love!' giggling when she came into the classroom. Bruce collected her from school the Friday afternoon before half-term, and she could sense the ripple of admiration and amazement as the girls took in his good looks and expensive car.

'Hello darling,' said Bruce, kissing her lightly as she got into the car. 'You look pretty. I've missed you so much.'

'Since yesterday?' she laughed softly to herself.

'It's seemed like an eternity, sweetheart.'

They planned to drive down by the river and eat in a small restaurant whose grounds sloped to the willowy water's edge. It was a picturesque setting and Eleanor was looking forward to some peace after her hectic day, and a romantic meal with Bruce.

He started the car and drove slowly out of the school grounds. 'Darling, I've some good news and some bad news. Which do you want first?'

'The bad news.'

'I'm sorry, but I have to break this date. Something really important has come up. There's a new Brazilian group who are going to be worth millions this time next year, and a certain American company are all set to sign them up. Well, I'm going to get to them first with an offer they can't refuse. I'm booked to fly to Rio tonight.'

'That's not such bad news,' said Eleanor, quickly hiding her disappointment. 'It's your job. I understand. Just take me home and I'll have a peaceful evening watching television and thinking of you flying to the sun. I'm quite envious . . .'

'Then you'll like the good news,' he said, quietly serious. 'When I return, we're going to get married. No more single trips. Next time I go abroad, you're coming with me.'

Eleanor's breath almost stopped at the suddenness of his proposal. He grinned and caught her hand.

'We can live in my flat or your house. Either would suit me – it's your choice. I travel about such a lot, I just need a base. And wherever you are is going to be my base.'

'Oh Bruce . . . ' Eleanor was lost for words. She tried not to think of her cats at that moment; she wanted to savour the joy and delight of knowing that Bruce wanted to marry her. And she need not move from her home. He was being so kind, not asking her to completely change her life-style. But if she married him, the cats would have to go . . . all four of them.

As he kissed her goodbye, she felt the stirring passion in his powerful arms. 'Not long, darling . . . ' he murmured.

Then he pulled away from her and slapped his hand against his breast-pocket. 'Oh God, I've forgotten my wallet!' He made a frantic search through his pockets. 'I went home and changed into this lightweight suit. Hell, I've left everything in my other suit . . . air ticket, travellers cheques, credit cards, currency. How much time have I got? I'll just make it back to my flat if I put my foot down. Sorry, darling, I must hurry if I'm going to catch that flight.'

He kissed her hastily. In that split second Eleanor saw his car, a crumpled, tangled wreckage on the hard shoulder of the motorway, its wheels spinning madly in the air. She saw rivulets of blood escaping through the shattered glass.

'For goodness sake, don't panic,' she said quietly. 'Come inside and I'll lend you the money.'

She herded the surprised cats into the kitchen, and Bruce followed her to the sitting room.

'Are you sure?' he asked. 'It's a lot of money. But it would be a great help. I hate cutting it fine, and I must get that flight. Tomorrow would be too late and the contract really is worth a fortune.'

'Of course you are going to make the flight,' said Eleanor. 'All in one piece.' She got her chequebook out of her desk. 'Now, how much will you need?'

'The plane ticket to Rio is £2,013. I'll be able to get a refund on the other one when I get back.'

'£2,013?'

'First class return, darling. I always travel first class. I need the leg room.'

'And your other expenses?'

'A couple of nights in a hotel, taxis, entertaining . . . say, another eight or nine hundred if you can manage it. The bank at the airport is open twenty-four hours a day. With your cheque to pay in, they'll let me have travellers cheques to the same amount and I'll use them to buy a new ticket. It's simple.'

'Are you sure?' Eleanor asked, writing the figures with a steady hand. 'I'll make it a round £3,000. A little extra for emergencies . . . '

'Darling, you're marvellous. You don't know how much I appreciate this.' His smile was warm and reassuring.

Eleanor felt almost married already as she handed him the cheque. There was no need for him to know that it would take all her savings. Anyway, it was only for a short time. He would pay her back as soon as he returned. She clung to him as he made to go.

When he had gone the house was very quiet. The four cats sat in the kitchen, not resentful but looking at her with resignation. Fu rubbed round her ankles, being the most forgiving of the four. She fondled his neck, feeling a lump of matted fur that reminded her that she had forgotten to groom them again. At least she could do that this evening. Cheynne jumped on the draining board, perking her head to one side, asking for a drink.

'My dear pussycats,' said Eleanor uncertainly as she fetched clean bowls and filled them with milk and water. 'What am I going to do about you? You are all so helpless. You depend on me, don't you? And you trust me . . . '

Eleanor could not sleep that night. She twisted and turned, thinking of Bruce flying high in the clouds, vulnerable in that tiny metal capsule. She heard one of the cats sneezing downstairs, and eventually, near dawn, she gave up trying to sleep and went down into the kitchen to heat some milk.

It was Chien. She was crouching in a dark corner, away from the other cats, sneezing, her eyes and nose running, an air of wearied despair in her trembling body. Eleanor was appalled by the change in her beautiful cat. She knew she had to act fast – cat flu could kill in a few hours. She would have to call the vet for some immediate treatment with antibiotics.

Quickly and gently she moved the sick cat into a box with clean blankets and placed it by the sitting-room fire. She tried to tempt the cat to drink, but Chien only hung her head over the bowl, uninterested.

'I'm sorry to call you out so early, but it's Chien,' said Eleanor on the telephone. 'I think she has flu.'

'I'll come right away,' said Arthur Dawes, the vet. He knew her cats well, and was a kindly man.

'You were right to call me,' he said later, washing his hands in the kitchen sink. 'Pneumonitis does respond to early treatment. But the recovery can be long and slow. I hope you feel up to nursing a sick cat – it's a time-consuming job if you are going to save her.'

'I don't mind that . . . but, well, I was going to have to think about finding new homes for all my cats,' said Eleanor in a small voice. 'For personal reasons.' She hid her face and bent to stroke Chien very lightly on the forehead. The cat was still very feverish.

'Completely out of the question at the moment, of course,' said the vet, packing away his equipment. 'And pretty dubious in the future, I should think. These cats are a family. You can't break them up. Chien would certainly die if you separated her from her sister. She would just give up. Cheynne too. By the way, have you ever thought of breeding from the Tortie? She's so unusual . . . ?'

As he was leaving, he gave her instructions for the next few hours. 'I want you to keep giving Chien a small quantity of glucose dissolved in warm water – it'll help to keep her going till the antibiotics take effect. I'll leave this medicine dropper with you, and I'll call round again later this morning after surgery.'

'You're very kind,' said Eleanor unsteadily.

'She's worth it. She's a lovely cat.'

By evening the fever was abating, but Chien was still very sick. Eleanor had her work cut out keeping her isolated from the other cats, who tried every means of slipping into the sitting room. Cheynne was desolate without her sister, searching restlessly through the house for her.

Eleanor lay back in a chair, exhausted by the long day, listening to Chien's laboured breathing. Her thoughts were in a turmoil. She could not decide what to do. As the light crept away, she switched on a low table lamp so as not to disturb Chien, and took a writing pad from the desk.

'My dear Bruce,' she wrote. 'This is the hardest letter I have ever had to write. Please try to understand how I feel, and that I have a responsibility which I took on and cannot give away just like an unwanted parcel. I know I am putting this badly . . . '

When the letter was finished, she put it in an envelope and left it in the hall. She did not have his full address. She knew he lived in a flat in the Barbican, but she did not have the number. She wanted to post it so that it would be there on his return from Brazil.

She refilled the medicine dropper with glucose water and fed it to Chien through the side of the cat's mouth. Drop by drop the liquid went in. Chien's eyes followed Eleanor's movements. She knew that Eleanor was saving her life. She lay on her side on the bed of blankets, wheezing, too weak to lift her head.

Later, as Chien's breathing got easier, Eleanor fell asleep curled up in a chair. Several times she woke to wipe away the mucus from the cat's nose and to feed her more sugary water.

Cheynne was awake too, padding around the kitchen. Eleanor was terrified that the other cats might develop the flu even though the vet had inoculated them – there were so many forms of the virus that it was difficult to give the correct vaccine.

Eleanor changed her shoes yet again, washed her hands, and went through to comfort the distressed Tortie. 'She's getting better,' she murmured, stroking the worried little face. 'You'll be able to see her soon.'

By Monday morning, Chien was definitely improving – her high temperature was coming down and she lapped a drop of milk. Eleanor was stiff and tired. She eased her neck and promised herself a hot bath after she had posted the letter.

She telephoned the renting office at the Barbican and

asked them to look up the number of Bruce's flat. The girl returned to the telephone some minutes later.

'I'm sorry but we don't have a tenant of that name. Perhaps it's some other block of flats.'

'I felt sure he said the Barbican,' said Eleanor, puzzled.

'Maybe he shares, and the flat is in another name.'

'That's probably the answer. Thank you. I'll contact his firm and get the number from them.'

Eleanor looked up the number of the record company and dialled it. The switchboard operator misunderstood her at first.

'Mr Leander? One moment please and I'll put you through to Mr Leander.'

'No, no. You've got the wrong name. Mr Lefant. Mr Bruce Lefant. I want to speak to someone who can give me Mr Lefant's home address.'

'I'll put you through to Personnel. One moment please.'

Personnel were mystified. There was no Bruce Lefant on their staff. Never had been. If she insisted they would check with Contracts. Rio? No, no one was representing them in Rio. Sorry, but they did not know of any Brazilian group which had a chance of making the British charts, let alone the American. . . someone must be pulling her leg.

Eleanor put down the telephone. Her hand was shaking. It was no joke. No joke at all. She picked up her letter and tore it into confetti. She knew that there was no need to send any letter. She would not be seeing Bruce again.

She felt physically sick. She wanted to crawl away and hide somewhere. The hurt was a stunning pain that made her want to die, to feel nothing any more.

She went through to the kitchen in a daze, not really knowing where she was or what she was doing. Mechanically she went through the motions of filling the kettle and putting it on the gas stove. Then she slid down on to the floor and wept.

Cy had been watching her from the top dresser shelf. Cy, the father cat, the big Blue Colourpoint who was really grey, who gave no concessions to anyone, who kept himself to himself.

Cheynne sat close by the sitting room door, her pretty

patched face still pleading for one glimpse of her sister. Fu was on the windowsill, watching a bee buzzing among the creeper outside. He longed to be let out to play, but he knew this was not the moment to ask.

Eleanor cried until she thought there could be no more tears left inside her. She searched her pockets for a handkerchief.

Silently the big Cy leaped down from the dresser and padded over to where Eleanor sat on the floor. She looked at him in surprise through blurred eyes. He had never come to her before.

Quite slowly, as if not totally sure of his welcome, he climbed on to her lap, a huge, heavy, warm, wonderful creature offering the only comfort he knew.

It was then that Eleanor realised she still had time to telephone her bank and stop the cheque. As the handsome Bruce had not been on his way to Rio, he would not have gone to the airport. He would be paying that cheque into his account this morning.

Eleanor sighed. He had made a mistake in underestimating her devotion to her family. Devotion which had made her write a letter.

But she did not rush to the telephone. She had to talk to big Cy for a few moments, to get to know him, to make the first overtures of friendship.

15 FELIS DOMESTICUS SURRENTUM

From the age of five Elisabeth Fiorentino had been singing. The daugher of an English schoolteacher and an Italian cellist, singing came as naturally to her as breathing and she was given every encouragement. As the years went by she progressed from 'Ding, dong, pussy's in the well' to 'The Sound of Music', till eventually she was studying Mozart at the Guildhall School of Music and famous arias floated from the open windows of her bedroom, soaring to the treetops like birdsong.

The world of music recognised her talent as her voice grew more beautiful, and she travelled extensively on singing engagements. But Elisabeth found that the dedicated life of an opera singer was a lonely one. She desperately needed company other than that of other professional singers or her business manager. Men seemed almost afraid of her – or of the effortless sounds that came from her throat, as if she were not quite human.

The few men who did enter her life did not stay long once they discovered how many hours went into the perfecting of each note and phrase. They could not compete with her discipline, nor did they care to take second place to a voice.

So cats became Elisabeth's friends and travelling companions. The first was called simply Fluffy, then, at intervals arrived Fluffy-Two, Fluffy-Three and Fluffy-Four. They were acquired and christened because of the strict quarantine laws of great Britain. When Elisabeth first flew abroad to sing *Tosca* at the Metropolitan Opera House in New York's Lincoln Centre, she took with her a pretty grey and white Persian kitten in a quilted travelling cat box. It was cold in New York with dirty snow piled high on the corners of the streets. But Elisabeth loved the towering skyscrapers and walked the full length of Fifth Avenue with her small friend, learning many things about that brash and bustling city.

But on Elisabeth's eventual return to England, Fluffy had to go into cat kennels at Tunbridge Wells for six months. Lonely and depressed, Elisabeth bought Fluffy-Two, a similarly enchanting kitten. The exercise repeated itself when Elisabeth was booked to sing in Zurich, and again when she went halfway across the world to sing in the butterfly-shaped Sydney Opera House.

She was now accompanied by Fluffy-Four and recuperating from an exhausting series of recitals in Italy culminating in a gala performance at La Scala. A doctor warned her not to sing for at least two weeks and she decided to stay at the Hotel Excelsior Vittoria in Sorrento, hoping that the gloriously rugged scenery of the peninsula and the heavenly blue of the sea would restore her jagged nerves and overtired vocal chords.

The fertile plain of Sorrento was a vast terrace above the sheer cliffs that fell into the Bay of Naples, acres of orange and lemon groves, walnut, fig, cherry and pomegranate trees. The villas intruded through the flowering greenery, red-washed, faded pink or white, civilisation encroaching on what nature had intended to be simply a huge garden. There were no beaches – sunbathing platforms stretched out to the sea for the tourists to invade.

Fluffy-Four, or Four, as he was more familiarly called, resented the jolting ride down the long, paved drive from the Piazza Tasso to the entrance of the hotel. It was ignominious to be perched on top of Elisabeth's matching hide luggage and wheeled in on a trolley by a porter. He protested loudly but no one took any notice.

Four could smell aromatic orange and lemon trees and he wanted to be out and exploring. Milan had been so boring. He yawned. Through the slits of his tartan-lined wicker travelling basket (Four detested tartan) he caught tantalising glimpses of trees dripping with orange and yellow globes, of Elisabeth's pastel mink coat swinging from her slender shoulders, of her mane of honey-coloured hair tied back with a silk scarf from Yves St Laurent. He miaowed again to attract her attention to his plight.

Elisabeth turned and took Four's basket off the trolley before her luggage disappeared into the lower depths of the rambling cliff-side hotel. It had once been three imposing villas built a century earlier, relics of another era, each clinging with fortress-like buttresses on impossible sites. Two were painted red, the third was a white palace. Now all three were married into one by somewhat haphazard additions of a Swiss-style chalet and a high, glass foyer and entrance. The foyer looked like a gilded bird cage with enough magnificent potted palms to house a whole aviary of exotic birds.

'I am Elisabeth Fiorentino,' said Elisabeth. 'You have my reservation. And I trust there is no objection to my cat.'

'None at all, Signorina Fiorentino. We are delighted to welcome such a famous singer to our hotel. We have reserved the Caruso room, or you may care to see the Princess Margaret suite? Her Royal Highness stayed here in May 1949.'

'And what about Four?'

'You want to see four rooms?'

'Four is my cat.'

'You have four cats?'

'Four is the name of my cat. He is one cat,' said Elisabeth patiently, knowing she must not raise her voice.

The manager had been trained not to show bewilderment. 'Pets are not allowed in the public rooms or in the restaurant,' he said. 'There will be a charge depending on size.'

'You mean you are going to measure him? From nose to tail, or side to side?'

'Is this a small cat or a large cat?' the manager queried.

'I should say he is a large small cat,' said Elisabeth, suddenly tiring. 'He is a small cat inside a lot of thick fur.'

Each of the villas was a period piece. Marble staircases

with pastel murals, grand master bedrooms, extensive balconies that took in panoramic views of the Bay of Naples, the majestic snow-tipped Vesuvius and the range of Lattari mountains.

The Caruso bedroom was a high-ceilinged confection of ornate gold and white marble, a vast gilt bed, full length brocade curtains billowing in the sea breezes, priceless pieces of furniture. Elisabeth imagined the bill if Four sharpened his claws on the legs of the antique desk and shook her head.

The Princess Margaret room was a corner sun-trap with three big windows opening on to balconies. It was large enough to hold a party in. Elisabeth and Four would be lost among the beautiful furniture, overpowered by the magnificent chandelier, awed by the palatial marble bathroom. Across a hallway that could be shut off was a private sitting room, again furnished with antiques. Elisabeth shook her head. Four yawned. He was used to this. Elisabeth was very particular about rooms.

'Perhaps one of our de luxe suites would be more suitable?' He thought . . . the Fiorentino suite would sound good.

The top floor suite in the white villa was far less overpowering – airy, more modern, with rugs on highly polished floors, a built-in wardrobe with painted flowers on the doors, a vast double bed, a luxurious bathroom across a small hallway, and, best of all, a completely private, walled, corner balcony overflowing with urns of flowers.

Quite nice, thought Four, jumping out of his detested basket and having a delicious stretch. He could smell the sea, fish, flowers and unknown herbs, and a shiver of excitement rippled along his fur.

Elisabeth laid her cheek on his velvety coat. 'I shall get better here,' she told him. 'We will sit in the sun and wander around and be just like other ordinary tourists.'

It sounded perfect to Four, especially sitting in the sun. He began to purr and nudge her chin. He wanted to get going.

But Elisabeth had to unpack first. Four helped. He attacked her fluffy swansdown slippers, hid under a pile of cashmere sweaters, had to fight to the death with a box of tissues. Finally he dragged a cobwebby shawl under a chair and trampled it into a new bed.

Elisabeth went on her knees and tugged at the shawl but his claws were firmly enmeshed in the wool. His eyes glinted with glee. He loved a tussle.

'Now you're being very naughty,' said Elisabeth sternly. It was a clash of wills that was resolved when there was a discreet knock on the door. A waiter had arrived with Four's supper served in special cat dishes, on a tray, and Elisabeth took the opportunity to disappear for her own. Four settled down to demolish flaked fish, freshly caught that morning in the Bay, artistically topped with curls of butter, unaware of the stir his beautiful mistress was making on her arrival in the elegantly-pillared dining room.

Waiters straightened their white jackets; the maître d'hotel immediately gave her the best window seat; diners stopped eating, forks in mid-air; heads swivelled to catch a glimpse. She was wearing a cream silk suit, pale and shimmering, her hair caught up in a loose knot with escaping tendrils, and dangling gold earrings.

Chester Ridgway had no inhibitions. As soon as Elisabeth had eaten and moved into the many-mirrored lounge to order coffee, he strolled over, one hand casually in the pocket of his dark blue velvet jacket. He was a handsome young man, not very tall, with curling brown hair touching his well-shaped ears; his half-closed blue eyes regarding Elisabeth with admiration.

'May I join you for coffee?' he asked, confident of his acceptability.

Elisabeth shook her head.

'But you should not be alone,' he said persuasively. 'A beautiful woman should always be complemented by the rugged contrast of male company.'

Elisabeth sighed faintly. She pointed to the small cigar smoking in his fingers and then to her throat. He apologised immediately.

'Of course, Miss Fiorentino, I should have been more thoughtful. I do apologise.'

Her heart fell. He had recognised her. Now she would

never get rid of him. She smiled distantly and again pointed to her throat, shaking her head in pantomime.

'Ah, I understand. You're resting that exquisite voice of yours. Then you are certainly in dire need of entertaining company,' said Chester, settling himself in the other deep armchair, and signalling to a steward. 'Two more coffees, a Drambuie and a Brandy Alexander. Ladies always like a Brandy Alexander,' he told Elisabeth, a hand sliding automatically into a pocket for his cigar case. 'My name's Chester Ridgway. I daresay you've heard of Ridgway Tiles? My father started the business just after the war. I'm a director, of course. I do a lot of travelling for the firm.'

So it seemed. There was hardly anywhere he had not been. He also knew all the local excursions from Sorrento, and seemed to think it was his mission in life to arrange her stay for her.

Elisabeth listened and sipped her frothy cream drink, wondering how she could politely take herself from this well-meaning but boring young man.

'And, of course, you mustn't miss the magnificent coastal drive to Positano and Amalfi. The views are quite splendid. Perhaps you would allow me to escort you?' he offered, his feeling of confidence growing as he marvelled at her flawless skin and tumbling tawny hair. She was a real catch.

Elisabeth shook her head and smiled politely. 'You are very kind but my husband is arriving tomorrow,' she whispered. She stood up. 'Thank you for the drink. Now I must take my cat for a walk. Good night.'

As an exit line, it was effective, whether it was the husband or the cat that did the trick, but she left Chester staring after her blankly.

The next day Elisabeth and Four set out to explore Sorrento at their leisure. They caused quite a stir. At first the Sorrentine shop-keepers were astonished and amused by the sight of the slight young woman leading a blue-grey cat on a lead. But then Elisabeth's sad brown eyes, almost hidden by her long fringe of honey hair, made each man sigh and long to bring a smile to her face. Four was universally admired by the women and petted by the children. And rightly so. He was a fine and proud Short-hair Blue-Cream Burmese, whose delicately shaded coat was like thick grey velvet. Four looked back at his admirers with large fierce eyes that reflected the elusive golden light of the Sorrentine sky.

Four strained at his lead. He was ecstatic with curiosity. Sorrento was definitely a cat place, and he could hardly contain his high spirits.

Leading from the Piazzo Tasso was the Via S. Cesareo, a narrow alley crowded with open-fronted shops. Glistening fresh fish lay on wet slabs within sniffing distance; goat cheeses swung from doorways; fruit was piled high in casual confusion still twigged with dark green leaves from the local groves.

A tortuous, twisting stone-stepped path led steeply through narrow old houses dating back to the fifteenth and sixteenth centuries, now festooned with twentieth-century washing, jeans, printed vests and drip-dry sheets.

Four's nose told him when they were nearing the Marina Grande, the original fishing harbour still cluttered with brightly painted fishing boats, yards of orange nets being repaired, and ragged children playing on the dark volcanic sand among dead fish, straggling seaweed and washed-up flotsam. Cats roamed in packs. Dozens of them. They glared at Four from under upturned rowing boats. He glared back, unafraid, a low hiss coming from his throat, thoroughly enjoying the sensation. It was a long time since he'd had a good hiss.

The little shore was bustling and noisy, cluttered with vehicles and boats, fishermen smoking and yarning and mending nets, women carrying their shopping and washing on their heads, children squabbling and chasing each other, barefooted and dirty. The closely built, red-roofed houses clung to the hillside, almost crowding out the fishermen's church on the front, cheek by jowl with dim taverns and bars, with hardly a postcard or souvenir in sight.

'The real Sorrento,' said Elisabeth, stepping carefully over the rubbish washed up on the cobbles by the night's rough seas. Four tugged hopefully in the direction of some fish-heads, but Elisabeth had glanced back and caught sight of Chester Ridgway descending down the same stone-stepped path, a suede jacket slung casually over his shoulders. It was no coincidence.

For a moment Elisabeth panicked. She darted along a lane and up some steps, only to find herself in someone's backyard among washing and crates. Another alley led to the landing of a house. Next she found herself facing a blank, sheer cliff face. Marina Grande seemed to be a labyrinth of alleyways leading nowhere. She did not want to go back the way she had come and meet Chester. The one road at the far end was a nightmare of revving mopeds, cars trying to turn, hooters blaring and no pavement. Four would be terrified out of his wits.

They were trapped, and Chester Ridgway was catching them up. He knew she could not escape. Any moment now he would stroll over, ready to pin her down with an invitation, arranging her day, planning her evening for her. At least he could see now that she really did have a cat.

A hefty fisherman's jersey suddenly blocked her way. Its owner side-stepped and started to stride away with purpose, as if he knew where he was going. His face was darkened by the sun, his grey hair roughened up by the wind, longish but well cut. Elisabeth spoke without thinking.

'Please can you help me?' She said it in English.

The man half turned and stopped. He did not look surprised, as if beautiful women were always asking him for help.

'But, of course. . . ' he said, a trace of accent in his voice.

'I'm lost. There are so many blind alleys. It's very confusing and I must get out quickly. Can you show me a back way up to the town?'

'There is the road. . . '

'My cat would be terrified and there's no pavement. Besides, I would be seen.'

Chester Ridgway had seen her. He raised an arm in salute and was rapidly negotiating a route between the drawn up fishing boats, trying not to step on unmentionable debris.

The colour drained from Elisabeth's face. She turned to the stranger, trying to glean his character from his face.

'Please. . . could you pretend to be my husband. . . just for a few moments?' she asked urgently, in a low voice. 'It's very important to me. . . '

It must have been the look of desperation in her eyes, for the stranger calmly took her arm and began to guide her from the harbour front. Chester was only a few yards away.

'Did you enjoy your walk?' the stranger said casually but loud enough for Chester to hear. 'The air is very refreshing. I thought you looked a little pale last night.'

'I was awfully tired,' said Elisabeth, racking her brains for some long-married conversational phrases. 'And I had a headache. But it's gone now. Did you get the shopping you wanted?'

'No. You know I don't enjoy shopping without you to help me choose.'

Elisabeth had a sudden feeling that the man was laughing at her, but his expression was quite serious.

'Hello there,' called Chester, beaming.

'Good morning,' said Elisabeth, then turned to her newly acquired husband. 'You're a little late, you know. I thought that any moment I was going to be shouted at in Italian for trespassing on private property.'

'Forgive me for keeping you waiting. . . ' He began to lead her through an archway then along a dank subterranean tunnel. It came out at some steep stone steps cut in the hillside, the back walls of houses shutting out the light. Four leaped up the steps agilely at the full length of his lead, easily keeping up with the man's long strides. By the time they reached the main road, Elisabeth was out of breath. But they had lost Chester on the way.

'Don't attempt that way on your own. Particularly at night.'

Elisabeth leaned against a wall, keenly aware that he was watching her. 'I couldn't even remember it, if I tried,' she said.

'Why do you keep your cat on a lead?' he went on.

'Because I'm afraid of losing him,' said Elisabeth. 'He is all I've got in the world.'

Four sat down and began to rearrange his fur with his pink tongue. He always felt slightly embarrassed when people began to talk about him. But he had enjoyed the chase up the hillside. He had not been quite sure what they were chasing, but it had been fun. He was not at all puffed. He hoped the man would take them somewhere else. . .

The man paused, taking in her expensive white trousers, cashmere sweater, the gold bangles jangling round her thin wrists. He seemed rough and shabby by contrast, but if Elisabeth had looked closely she would have seen that his hands were strong but not coarsened by hard manual labour. Nor was he as old as his greying hair might indicate. His accent was clipped, faintly Germanic.

'You look as if you have got everything,' he said shrewdly.

Elisabeth recognised that they were at the other end of Corso Italia, the main street. She now knew her way back to the hotel.

'Thank you for helping me.'

He nodded briefly. 'My pleasure. Anytime you have need of a husband. Bar Genny makes good coffee. Ciao.'

The man walked away without a further look. The idea of some coffee was tempting so she crossed the road to the unpretentious little café. It was crowded with locals leaning against the bar in the pleasant steamy atmosphere, talking or watching the portable television behind the bar. Thick white cups stood in a deep tray of hot water. The customers looked at her curiously, but after a first admiring glance, returned to their gossip.

The man was right. The cup of cappuccino arrived piping hot, delicious tasting with powdered chocolate sprinkled on the frothy top.

Four had seen something interesting: two lads were playing a machine which had white spots of light bouncing around and was making bleeping sounds. It was fascinating. He was mesmerised by the bobbing lights. Someone found him a stool and he jumped up on it to be nearer the game. The youths were amused by the cat's interest and put in more 100-lire coins so that they could play another match for him to watch.

Four was mesmerised, tense and excited, his eyes gleaming. Eventually he could resist the balls no longer. His paw shot out, making wild swipes at the bleeping lights. He sat back on his haunches, frantic paws windmilling like a drunken boxer. Elisabeth began to laugh at the cat's antics – it was the first time she had laughed for months.

That evening Elisabeth sat alone at her table in the dining-room, listening to the uncanny boom of the waves lashing at the rockface below, but without being able to see anything out of the darkened windows. The weather was changing. She briefly acknowledged Chester's wave, then pretended to be absorbed in admiring the vaulted ceiling painted blue with pastoral scenes of cherubs and angels. Very Florentine. Rain spattered the paved terrace outside the windows. The night was black and chilly with only the string of flickering lights across the Bay to show that at least Naples was alive.

A howling wind tore at the cliffside. No wonder the lemon and orange groves were protected from the lashing winds and winter frosts by acres of untidy bamboo mats and cages.

Elisabeth did not linger but quickly took Four for a walk along the paths that crossed the groves of the hotel's garden. Four did not like rain, and trod fastidiously over the puddles with delicate steps.

Elisabeth stood in the midst of the gale, the scarf round her precious throat being whipped away, streaming behind her. She wondered what she was doing there. Totally alone. She was famous and successful, but no one cared about her. She could disappear tomorrow and in days she would be forgotten. When she returned to the glass foyer, the kindly hall porter who opened the door did not know whether they were tears or raindrops on her cheeks.

The next morning the sky had miraculously cleared and from her breakfast table Elisabeth saw the white steamer coming from Capri. Her spirits lifted. Already a small crowd had gathered on the landing stage at the promise of a fine day and a good crossing. Elisabeth hastily swallowed her sweet roll and coffee, then hurried to fetch Four. He looked at her inquiringly as she bundled him into his travelling basket. No brush and comb this morning?

'We're going to Capri,' she whispered. 'Let's get the lift. We've just got time.'

Four did not care for the motion of the steamer, but he bore it with fortitude, sitting at Elisabeth's feet on the top deck. She found the forty-five-minute trip bracing and exciting, and her cheeks were flushed as the *Epomeo Napoli* reversed between the towering cliffs into the quay at the Marina Grande. No wonder people fell in love with Capri and returned time after time. The harbour was still small enough to be picturesque. Houses straggling up the verdant hillside in colourful profusion, the curves and soft corners of their beaten plaster walls merging with the flowers.

The steep funicular railway was a new sensation for Four, accustomed as he was to air and car travel. He was quite surprised to find how high up he was when Elisabeth took him out of his basket on the paved terrace of the hilltop town of Capri, overlooking the Marine Grande. The sea was a long way down, beyond the carpet of faded roofs and gnarled olive trees, the waves sparkling with a special luminosity.

The small, oddly-shaped Piazza Umberto I was bustling with warmly-dressed locals and cosmopolitan visitors, even though it was not the summer season. The rash of mink coats was quite startling in such a quaintly old-fashioned square, for despite the expensive dress shops and trendy boutiques in the sprouting alleyways, much of the town's eighteenth-century character was untouched. Remains of a megalithic wall were visible by the funicular railway, going mostly unnoticed and unrecognised, built into existing houses.

Elisabeth wandered into a narrow passage. She should have known it. There was Chester. He was obviously on the tourist trek to Anacapri and the famous Villa S. Michele. Elisabeth immediately chose the opposite direction, following the Via Fuerlovado to Caesar Tiberius's ruined villa on the top of Mount Tiberio. The Roman *stradetta* was only wide enough for two people to pass, covered part of the way, occasionally broadening at crossroads. The route was clearly marked with coloured ceramic tiles or the inscription 'Villa Jovis' on marble.

She climbed higher, Four leaping ahead. A twisting path took them between villas and gardens, steep enough to become steps on the bends, glorious views of the island behind and in front of them as the extensive ruins came into sight.

The last few hundred yards were all steps. She sat on a tiled base of the Imperial loggia, getting her breath, leaning her back against the cold white stone. Four lay stretched out in the sun like an emperor himself. It was still and peaceful, the sweet silence broken only by an occasional firecracker being let off by late New Year revellers. Some German students clustered beneath the greened bronze statue of a saintly Maria del Soccorso, their clear young voices not disturbing the stillness, but reassuring her that ghosts of Roman senators, togas flapping, would not stride out of the baths below, demanding that she serve wine and figs immediately.

Elisabeth understood the ageless magic of Capri. The island seemed so light, as if it were a ship moving on the oceans. Cliffs fell dramatically to the sea on both sides and, beyond the slopes, rose again dotted with tiny villas, their dark windows like cubic eyes.

The ruins of the Villa Jovis sprawled across the whole hilltop, once a dominating fortress, but now the towering stone walls were hardly recognisable as the great hall, the baths – hot, cold and tepid. A mass of stairways, terraces and promenades linked the roofless rooms, descending to the more prosaic living quarters, kitchens and sewers.

A dog had followed the workmen as they cemented the present path and 162 steps for tourists, writers and lonely singers. Its paw-marks were imprinted in the cement, more real to Elisabeth than the great Caesar Tiberius who had once strode on this same loggia, contemplating his retirement from the complicated politics of his office.

'And how is your marital situation today?' the man asked, coming into sight as he climbed the crumbling steps to the loggia.

'Safe and single at the moment,' said Elisabeth. 'But I have a feeling I may need a husband on the return ferry.'

'Then perhaps I should get in a little practice,' he said, and again she did not know if he were serious or teasing her. 'How do you explain why we are not staying at the same hotel?'

'I don't know,' she faltered. 'I had not thought it out that far.'

'We could pretend that I am allergic to your cat.' Elisabeth shot a quick glance at him, but he was calmly taking in the magnificent view. 'Nasal or skin?'

'I beg your pardon?'

'Sneezing or lumps? The allergy. . . '

Elisabeth bent down to hide her amusement by touching Four's soft, velvety head. 'Four wouldn't give anyone lumps!'

'I think perhaps you should tell me your name. I cannot call you darling all the time, however delightful that is.'

'Elisabeth. Elisabeth Fiorentino.'

'Mixed parentage? That explains the Italian eyes and the Anglo-Saxon colouring. But not your cat on a lead. Poor cat.'

'He's not a poor cat,' she said defensively. 'I can do what I like with Four. It's a free world.'

'But not for your cat. Your cat is a prisoner.' He lifted the slack of the lead with the toe of his sandal. Four stirred and stretched, and rolling over to warm his other side, claws retracting. He liked this man's voice. He knew who it was without opening his eyes. He hoped there would be another exciting chase. . .

'I don't agree,' said Elisabeth, but guilt had crept into her voice. She knew playful, amusing Four was soon destined for six-months' captivity in a kennels where her other cats still languished. Fluffy-One's quarantine had expired and Elisabeth would fetch her as soon as she arrived back in England. But her agent had already signed up another overseas engagement – Elisabeth had no choice but to start the cat on the same merry-go-round. 'No, I don't agree,' Elisabeth repeated very firmly.

'The cat is a symbol of liberty,' said the man, still gazing into the far shimmering hills. 'The Roman goddess of liberty always has a cup in one hand, a broken sceptre in the other and a cat lying at her feet. You don't know freedom, eh, puss?'

'You're talking about statues. Carved pieces of marble. What nonsense! They mean nothing.' Elisabeth was not used to being lectured.

'You can't say that, in Italy of all places. Tomorrow you should go to see Pompeii. I will take you.'

'You sound like Chester.'

'Then you are making yourself a prisoner also.'

'But I am already. A prisoner of my career.'

He walked over to the edge of the loggia. The ruins scattered down the hillside, overgrown with weeds and flowers, almost unreconisable as the luxurious Roman villa.

'We only come to this earth once,' he said, almost to himself. 'My name is Hans Johanson. I am Swiss. This much you should know about your husband. Shall we walk now?'

They walked back down the 162 steps, strolling through orchards and olive groves, flowering oleanders spilling on to the path. Hans told her about the famous people who had villas on Capri. Everyone knew about Gracie Fields and her swimming pool restaurant at Marina Piccola, but Elisabeth was surprised that Ginger Rogers also had a villa. . . bright haired, ageless, still dancing. Others who had lived there included the Marquis de Sade, Gorky, Chaliapin, Tchaikovsky, Alex Munthe, D.H. Lawrence, and now modern industrialists who made their fortunes from household products had moved in.

A terraced bar overlooked a steep downward path. Plain wooden tables were laid out in the open. The cooking was done in a cave, rock walled; a woman and her daughters were chopping food on boards. Aromatic smells wafted from their cooking pots.

Elisabeth and Hans ordered a simple spaghetti Neapolitan with a bottle of local red wine. The elderly man who served them brought a dish of fish pieces for Four, and a bowl of water, without being asked. 'We have no milk,' he apologised.

Later they walked down the twisting steps, every turn presenting an even more magnificent view. They came to the Arco Naturale, a soaring archway formed in the limestone rock by slow erosion. The arch rose into the sky, but by moving to different angles, Elisabeth could look through the eye of the arch and see a vista of receding pools, each bluer than the other, unbelievably still. Four leaped on to the low wall of the viewing point, the wind ruffling his velvet coat into wavelets.

Hans was standing close behind Elisabeth. He bent unexpectedly and kissed her. It was a kiss without passion, but with a gentleness that stirred a quiver of emotion in Elisabeth's heart.

They were quite alone. They had the island to themselves. The crystal moment was handed them by the Gods.

'Just practising. . . for the return trip,' said Hans lightly, but the intensity of his expression did not match the lightness of his voice. He was searching for something he could not find. His dark eyes were unfathomable. Elisabeth found she was shaken to her very roots.

An American family joined them on the return ferry. They had two miniature-adult, crew-cut small sons and had saved for a long time for this trip to Europe.

The father was resigned to their tour operator's lightning itinerary, but still American enough to make fun of it.

'We had ten minutes of Capri,' he said. 'Or was it twelve? My wife dashed into one shop, I went into another. We threw our money on the floor and shouted "Give us something!" '

Hans and Elisabeth laughed. 'If only you had come with us,' said Hans. 'My wife and I had a most enjoyable walk up to the Roman villa on the top of the hill.'

It was almost like a stab. Elisabeth had to steady herself against the rail. He had said it so naturally, words that she had never expected to hear. Even though it was a pretence, they kindled a tiny glow within her.

Capri was slipping away from them in the distance. It had been a wonderful day, and she did not want it to end. It was cooling fast and the passengers began to crowd into the steamy cabin. She did not know which would be the most harmful, the chill wind or the incubating germs in the cabin. It had seemed pretentious to go to Capri in a mink coat, but she was shivering now. Always her voice. She must not do this, or that. . . she must cosset it, care for it. The voice was more real than she was. Elisabeth Fiorentino was simply a shell that housed the precious chords. . .

'You are cold, darling,' said Hans, draping his anorak on her shoulders and zipping it up high under her chin. She immediately felt the warmth it still held from his body.

'How about you?' She was lost inside its size.

'I am like Four. I have an in-built wind resistance. Remember, I am used to mountains and snow.'

'You must be a skiing instructor,' said Elisabeth, reminding herself of everything she had heard about skiing instructors.

'Wrong. But be careful. Your admirer approaches.'

Chester was bearing down on them, two brandies in his hand. He looked momentarily disconcerted to find Hans with Elisabeth, the wind spraying her hair across his chest in tangled locks.

'Oh. So you're the husband. You do exist then,' said Chester. 'I was beginning to wonder.'

'Most certainly,' said Hans, shifting slightly so that he shielded her from the wind. 'I exist.'

'I thought you might like a brandy,' Chester turned to Elisabeth. 'It could get rough. I'm feeling a bit queasy myself.'

'What a kind thought,' said Elisabeth, feeling safe now that Hans was with her. 'I'm sorry you don't feel well. You must stay in the fresh air.'

'Not staying at the Excelsior, are you?' Chester probed.

'No. Unfortunately I am allergic to my wife's cat.'

'Sneezes,' said Elisabeth.

'Lumps,' said Hans.

They both spoke at the same time and Chester could not understand why they started to laugh. It did not seem at all funny to him.

'What happens when you are at home?' he went on. 'You

don't live in separate houses, do you? All for a cat?'

Elisabeth smiled sweetly at Hans. He could deal with that one. But he was not lost for an answer.

'No, at home, it is the cats who have a separate house. Not me. Just like some people have a granny-flat, we have a cats-flat. Is it four cats we have, darling?' Hans sounded suitably confused.

'Four,' Elisabeth confirmed.

Hearing his name, Four called out from his basket. His fierce amber eyes were watching everything. Elisabeth stroked his chin. He was a beautiful cat. He deserved more than the kind of life she was committing him to, but what else could she do?

It was dark when the ferry reached the quay below the hotel, its windows bright with lights like a many-layered birthday cake. Hans took her arm and guided her across the swinging gangway. The waves were washing over the landing stage and they ran to higher, dryer land. They walked back to the hotel along the winding Via de Maio that climbed the narrow ravine. They were strangely silent. The Piazzo Tasso was bustling with café customers sipping drinks, and Neapolitan music floated into the evening air.

'Will you be all right?' he hesitated at the drive.

'I think I can handle Chester now that he knows you really exist,' said Elisabeth, the words almost choking her. They were not what she wanted to say at all.

'I'm planning to catch the 9.55 train to Pompeii tomorrow, if you need me.' He touched her hand lightly, briefly.

Chester wanted to take her up to the crater of Vesuvius, and spent most of the evening trying to persuade her to go with him. 'Craters are just not my scene,' she kept refusing.

He followed her from the dining-room into the lounge. They made a handsome couple, reflected in the gilt mirrors on the walls. The romping, round-cheeked cherubs were still absorbed in their everlasting game of draping garlands of rosebuds from mirror to mirror. How solid everything was. . . cast iron free-standing radiators decorated with scrolls, almost museum pieces; even the blanking nut was faced with petals of a flower. The handles of the tall glass doors opening on to the terrace were the two halves of an oyster shell. Everywhere were signs of long lost workmanship. . . .

'You can't come to Sorrento and not see Vesuvius,' Chester insisted. He waved over the steward to give his order.

'I can see Vesuvius from my balcony,' said Elisabeth. 'Besides, I am going to Pompeii with my husband tomorrow.'

'I don't understand this marriage of yours,' said Chester.

'Hans is allergic to Four. It's quite simple.'

'It's a ridiculous arrangement,' he said laconically. 'Get rid of your cats. Or get rid of your husband – I daresay you would soon find a replacement who even liked cats.'

'I find that remark offensive,' said Elisabeth rising. 'Goodnight, Mr Ridgway.'

Elisabeth locked the door of her room and took Four up into her arms. It was so silly to be upset by Chester, when she did not even have a husband. She had even started to think that Hans. . . 'Oh Four, I wish you were a big fierce Alsatian dog to guard me,' she said vehemently. Four felt a tremor of alarm. He didn't like the idea of dogs at all.

He was even more alarmed when Elisabeth hurried to the Circumvesuviana station the next morning. He was jolted about in his basket and had to protest loudly before she slowed down.

'Oh, I thought I might miss you,' she said as a tall figure, reassuringly familiar, came from the booking office.

'I came early,' said Hans. 'I have bought two tickets. It's quite a short journey really. Ah, I forgot my duty. . . good morning, darling. Did you sleep well?'

He took her hand quite naturally. It felt warm, firm and comforting. Elisabeth had a heady feeling, as if she were suddenly sixteen again, and singing was no more than a girlish daydream.

Pompeii was a humbling experience. The splendid Roman city still lived on in all its pomp of long ago – when senators strode among the columns of the great Forum, the Roman ladies took the baths, servants tended the lordly villas, townsfolk sold wine and baked bread, the priests prayed, the gladiators fought their bloodied battles in the vast amphitheatre.

Elisabeth found it affected her deeply, especially the small things – the worn stepping-stones across the cobbled streets, the deep ruts made by the chariot wheels, the ancient graffiti scrawled in red dye on the walls, small household articles found intact in the ashes. . . bottles, pots, combs, tear phials. . .

A guide took them round the better preserved villas which were protected from the general public.

'Oh, it is locked,' he exclaimed theatrically outside an ornamental portico. 'I have forgotten the key. The key is with my brother who is visiting a sick aunt in Padua. . . ' His face was as wrinkled as an old walnut.

Hans put his hand casually in his wallet and pulled out some torn lire notes. The guide's expression lightened.

'Ah . . . ' he sighed with elaborate relief. 'Of course, I have, after all, another key in this pocket. Come . . . '

Four followed curiously. He loved exploring but he knew something was desperately wrong here in this strange hollow place of broken walls and crumbling marble columns. The volcanic ash still lingered in cracks and crevices, with all its sense of imminent death and disaster. He kept close to Elisabeth, getting right under her feet, to feel safer.

Hans caught her from stumbling. She picked Four up and he dug his claws sharply into her skin. 'You are in a funny mood,' she chided.

Suddenly a Roman deluge began. Vesuvius was lost in cloud. They ran for shelter to the cloisters of the gymnasium, which at least had a roof. The Grand Palestra had housed the crowds watching athletic feats held round the now empty marble-walled pool. Rain poured through gaps in the roof. Elisabeth wandered away from Hans, trying to bring her thoughts under control. Her heart was aching. This quiet man was stirring emotions in her that had lain hidden for years. It seemed she knew every line of his face, every curve of his shoulders, every inflection of his accent.

Through the grill of a wooden side-door, a small figure lay on its back in the grey dust, its skull broken open. It looked very small. A femur lay on the ground alongside. Other bones were piled in the dust. As Elisabeth's eyes grew accustomed to the gloom of the storeroom, she saw with horror that the yellow plastic trays were stacked with bones. Excavations were still being carried out. She shivered and hurried back to Hans.

'Your boyfriend is following us,' said Hans.

'I thought he'd gone to Vesuvius.'

Chester appeared at the far end of the cloisters, waving a large, coloured golf umbrella. The rain dripped off his brown curls, making him look like a Greek god in modern dress.

'Are you sure you still want me to act the husband?' Hans asked dubiously. 'He really is a most attentive young man, and he does have a very capacious umbrella.'

'I'd rather get wet,' said Elisabeth, tucking Four inside her jacket and pulling up the zip so that only his furry face was showing. He flattened his ears in disapproval of this whole rain business. He did not mind being carried about like an Eskimo baby, but he had a feeling he was still going to get very wet. He eyed the bright umbrella weaving its way towards them. It seemed a sensible solution. As Chester neared, Four did an elaborate gyration and slithered out from the bottom of Elisabeth's jacket. With one bound he cleared the nearest puddle, scrambled up Chester's suede coat and clung on to his shoulders.

'Ouch! Get off! Drat the creature!' Chester felt Four's claws dig into his neck. He tried to shake the cat off its perch, but Four was not going and hung on to Chester, his back arched, his wet fur spiked like a porcupine.

'Four, come down at once,' said Elisabeth sharply, but inwardly she was laughing at Chester's predicament. The umbrella rolled wildly, sailed out of Chester's hands and landed wrong-way up in a rushing stream of water. Hans waded after it as it drifted away like a gaudy boat.

Chester was nearly doubled over, trying to dislodge Four, almost blinded by the rain, staggering from one slippery ridge to the next. Four felt decidedly unsafe and with his usual quick thinking leaped back into the shelter of the cloisters, picking up his paws and shaking them delicately.

'You are in disgrace,' said Elisabeth, catching him up into her arms. 'I'm ashamed of you.' Four was not at all taken in by the tone of her voice. It had all been great fun, and he felt better for it. Now Hans had the umbrella and that meant it would soon be sheltering Elisabeth. He poked a wet nose into Elisabeth's ear, asking forgiveness.

'You'd better have the umbrella,' said Chester, wet and practically choking. 'Because of your precious voice. . . '

'Thank you, how kind. Perhaps we had all better get back to Sorrento,' she said hurriedly. 'This rain looks permanent.' Hans was looking at her strangely. 'What does he mean about your voice. . . ?' his eyes were saying. The journey back to Sorrento was strained. A chill settled on the group and they were silent. Elisabeth looked out of the train window at the grey suburban flats and houses and wondered where the colour of Italy had gone.

On her last evening in Sorrento Elisabeth sang in the cathedral. Three professors from Naples were to give a recital in the warm toned, pink and brown marble church, and when they heard that Elisabeth Fiorentino was staying at the Excelsior, they asked her to sing just one aria.

She sang the Easter Hymn, her voice soaring to the vaulted ceiling like a bird's, while the chandeliers shone and twinkled like stars in the heavens. Hans sat unseen in a pew at the back, Four curled up beside him. Hans did not know how he would be able to live without her. Each flawless note took her further and further away from him, underlining the difference in their lives.

Afterwards, as they walked slowly back to the hotel, she told him about her singing, about her career, her loneliness and her many cats. Tomorrow she would be flying back to England.

'Now is the time for our divorce then,' said Hans. 'Tomorrow you return to being the big star, Four will begin his six-months' quarantine, and I suppose next week you will go shopping to Harrods for number five.'

'Oh Hans,' said Elisabeth, shocked and hurt. 'What a cruel thing to say.'

'But it is true. You are using your cats as you would not dare to use a human. Or do you also cast off human relationships as quickly when they have finished their usefulness?'

'Why are you talking to me like this?' Elisabeth cried. 'Why are you being so unkind?'

'Because you have finished with me too. I am cast off like Four. I am fallen in love with you, Elisabeth, but I know it is no use. Our lives take different paths. You know nothing about me . . . I am a farmer. I have a small farm in the mountains. I work in the open air. We make good cheese. My house is of logs and when the snow comes there is no way down to the village. Sometimes I do not see another person for weeks. It is not your world at all. . . '

She was crying silently. Of course, it was true. How could she have thought, even for a moment, that Hans could fit into her life as a singer? But that kiss on Capri had been a miracle, when she had despaired of ever feeling love stirring within her.

'I'm not really like that,' she whispered. 'I don't want to leave you. Hans. . . please help me.'

Her eyes swam with tears as she fumbled with the collar round Four's neck. She picked the cat up and hugged him ferociously, kissing his soft grey forehead, stroking his ears with trembling fingers. It was a long moment when time seemed to stop.

Then she put him down on the paved path between the orange and lemon trees whose sharp fragrance drifted in the wind. 'There you are, Four. You're free. No nasty cage for my beautiful puss.'

Four shook himself. It felt strange without his collar. He had never been without that narrow leather strap before. The air lifted his fur and ruffled his neck. He turned himself round Elisabeth's ankles lovingly, and licked her hand with his rough moist tongue.

Then with one bound he was away. He knew where he was going. He streaked out of the hotel drive and down the Via S. Cesareo. His nose led the way. A right turning took him past the fourteenth century cloisters of Saint Francisco, down the cobbled steps to the Marina Grande. All the grand, tantalising smells of the harbour wafted up to meet him.

A quiver of excitement rose in his throat. This was to be his life now! He was free. . .

These days Four lives with a pack of half-wild cats that roam the harbour, well established as their leader. Often he can be seen sunning himself on the keel of an upturned boat, a beautiful Short-Haired Blue-Cream, a little out of place among the mixed breeds but obviously well-fed and content with life as a Neapolitan gipsy. And there are quite a few younger cats playing around him with a definite look of Blue about them.

Elisabeth and Hans come back to Sorrento regularly. It is their special place for holidays and the odd weekend break from her singing engagements. It took Elisabeth over a year to decide to marry Hans, but she found it was not so difficult after all to combine her career with being a farmer's wife. She can commute from Zurich easily. She loves Hans' log-built farmhouse in the mountains and the clear, sweet summer air is marvellous for her voice. But the time she likes best is when the snows come and there is no way down to the village. The fir-clad slopes stand white and silent, and she and Hans are together.

Chester returned to the Rome headquarters of the Italian police to whom he was on temporary loan. His next assignment was less glamorous – a wealthy Brazilian industrialist and his wife who were visiting Rome. The Italian Government, concerned by the number of kidnappings and ransoms that plagued their country, took what steps they could to protect potential victims.

Four always seems to know when Elisabeth and Hans are returning to Sorrento for a visit. His special sixth sense wakes him from his sun-baked slumbers, and, leaving his large family to tumble on the sands, he bounds through the back alleys up to the Piazzo Tasso. Then as their car turns into the drive of the Excelsior Vittoria, he emerges nonchalantly from the flowering bushes as if he has been there all the time.

Then, of course, Elisabeth rushes from the car, gathering him into her arms and covering him with joyous kisses and tears.

Four always stays at the hotel with them. He enjoys the occasional taste of luxury, but he knows that it is like all holidays. It is not real life. And for every cat, life is liberty.